A KILLER'S LOVE SERIES BOOK THREE

JENNIFER IVY

Dedication

For readers that like their morally grey man a little darker, meet Ajax.

TRIGGER WARNINGS

This book is a Dark Romance, and as such may contain subject matters, content, or events that you may find disturbing.

This includes but is not limited to:

Dubious Consent (Dubcon)

Blood

Gore

Kidnapping

Forced Proximity

Spanking

Breeding Kink

Bondage

Orgasm Control/Denial

Graphic descriptions of Violence, Torture, and Murder.

A KILLER'S LOVE SERIES BOOK THREE

JENNIFER IVY

CHAPTER ONE

Ajax

"Okay, Piglet, time to go," I say without glancing down at my daughter, making sure to keep my voice light and cheery, the exact opposite of what my body is. I'm tense, my body on full alert as my eyes track the man farther up the aisle.

I knew what he was the minute we locked eyes. It's written all over his face. The way his eyes assess those close, the way he tracks anyone walking into the aisle, the way his body shifts as his woman moves. His face pales slightly as we hold our gaze. He sees what I see.

We're the same.

He's a killer . . . like me.

He walks his woman to the other end of the aisle, but it's still too close for my liking.

He's tall and broad, but I'm stronger, and while

I'd like to avoid it at all costs, I'm not above killing a man in a grocery store.

Anything to protect Piglet.

"Daddyyy," Mary whines, drawing my attention. She lolls her head back far enough to pout at me without turning. My gaze flickers between her and the man leaving. *We need to leave.*

Placing my hand on the back of her head, I tilt it until she's standing straight and facing the cereal we stepped into the aisle for. "Mary Lou, it's time to go," I repeat, glancing down at her briefly.

Her little shoulders sag.

A smile creeps onto my lips. I give one last look down the now empty aisle, happy that Mary is safe for now. I crouch down behind my daughter, then reach out to take hold of the end of her pigtail. Twisting her waist-length hair, I tickle her under the chin with it. Mary squeals, and her smile melts away some of my anxiety.

"You can have those," I say, pointing at the obnoxiously bright and sugary-looking cereal box she's been eyeing for the last few minutes. "But then we are leaving."

I watch as Mary squints, looking at me through narrowed eyes. She twists her lips left to right, and I know she's about to fleece me.

"I get to pick two things from the checkout." She tries to bargain.

"One," I counter.

"Deal," she rushes, offering me her small hand.

2

Giving me a grin that I know mirrors my own, Mary shakes my hand with an enthusiasm that says she thinks she won. She didn't. I'd have crumbled if she doubled down at two items. *Anything to get us the fuck out of here.*

"You're too good at this. How are you only five?" I huff, feeding her pride.

"I know!" She smiles up at me.

God, I love her.

Chuckling, I twirl my finger above her head, and she spins instantly. Gripping her under her arms, I lift her to the top shelf so she can retrieve the cereal before safely placing her back down.

Using one hand to hold our cart, I reach out the other for my baby girl to take. With her hand secure in mine and the large box clutched tightly to her chest, Mary lets me lead her to the nearest checkout, a few tills away from him.

The length of the queue makes me groan. *So much for a quick escape.*

Keeping Mary close as we shuffle forward, I bite the inside of my cheek, pushing down the urge to tap my foot.

Finally, within reach of the conveyor belt, I try to distract Mary from the Halloween candy that's now brightly marked as on sale. The last thing this child needs is more candy. Her Halloween haul had been an epic success.

The corners of my mouth tip up. She did make a very cute pig.

Pulling the cart closer, I ask, "Baby, can you come help Daddy, please?"

Mary sighs like only a dramatic five-year-old can. I find myself fighting another smile. My mouth twitches, but I keep a straight face. I won't encourage her sass, no matter how cute it is.

Grabbing the few items we managed to get out of the cart one by one, I pass them over for her to place on the belt along with her cereal, which she does with care, shifting our purchases until she's happy with their placement. *Hmm,* maybe my OCD is rubbing off on her a little too much.

Shit.

Keeping our lives and the things in them clean and precise help me be the man I am, but I don't want that for Mary. I want my daughter to be better than me—happy, healthy, and stress-free.

Satisfied our last item is balanced and neat, Mary turns to me.

I grin. "Perfect, thank you."

Her sweet face smiles up at me, happy with the praise. Remembering my promise, I nod to the shelves just behind the conveyor belt. "You get one item," I remind her. After a small squeal, she's perusing for her next treat.

Please don't pick candy, I pray as she hems and haws over what she wants.

My gaze flits over to where the man and his woman had been, and they're still there. His face is drawn into a frown. Looks like I'm not the only one impatient to get out of here. *Good*, that means he doesn't want any trouble either.

Mary lifts her arm, her prize held up for me to see. A small rubber ball. *Perfect*. It'll keep her busy while I look at where we can head next since staying in Cromwell Town is no longer an option.

"That's a great choice, Piglet." I praise with a bright smile.

A bored-looking teenager starts to scan our items, shoving them to the bagging section with little care.

"Hi, welcome to Cromwell and Greene Grocery. How are you doing today?" he asks in a drab and monotone voice. The kid really hates his fucking job. *Fair*.

"Good, thanks," I answer, bagging our things quickly. He doesn't care that I'm about to have a fucking heart attack if I don't get my daughter out of a building that holds another killer.

Mary hands him her ball to be scanned, then hurries the few steps to stand on the right side of the scanner where the kid has been throwing our stuff. I chuckle when her little body slams into my leg.

So impatient and uncoordinated.

My baby girl grins up at me, pushes off my leg, and stretches her arm out to take her treat back from the cashier. Her smile fades quickly when the little prick carelessly throws it down to the end of the counter, past where I'm standing.

Instead of being stopped by the walled edge of the counter, like our bread and milk were, the ball bounces a few times, shoots off the end, hits the floor, and rolls between the feet of people heading for the exit.

Panic grips my heart when the sound of little feet running hits me at the same time that her small body zooms past me.

"Mary!" I snap, but she pays me no mind. Focused only on her runaway ball, she's oblivious to me rushing after her.

"Hey, you gotta pay!" the kid behind the counter shouts.

I don't answer, too busy snatching my daughter by the back of her jacket. The pink denim holds strong in my fist. Lifting her slightly, I draw in a deep breath and try to calm my pounding heart.

One more deep breath and Mary's feet touch the ground again as I set her down gently. Turning her toward me, I crouch in front of her.

I push my gray baseball cap up slightly, needing her to see how serious I am. "We've discussed you running off before. There's a lot of people here. What were you thinking?"

Wide blue eyes blink back at me for a few seconds before she tearily answers, "I just wanted my ball." Her little thumb points behind her at the still rolling toy.

I give another deep sigh. Standing, I offer my hand, squeezing her fingers when she takes it. Together, we weave between the other customers until we're close to the runaway item.

Stretching my leg out, I block the path of the ball. Mary is quick to take advantage of that, scooping up the ball and clutching it tight in her left hand.

And just like that, her smile is back. *At least one of us is happy.* My heart is still pounding, something that only gets worse when I look over to where the other killer had been . . . he and his girl are gone.

Shit.

Another dangerous man in the building is one thing, but not knowing exactly where he is, is another thing entirely.

We need to leave now.

Rushing back over to where I abandoned our shopping, I frown when I see two security staff approaching.

"Is there a problem here?" one asks, looking just as bored as the cashier had. The same little prick who's now sitting up straight, arms crossed with a look on his face that says he thinks he found one of America's most wanted. *If he only knew.*

"He rushed off without paying." He points at me.

"And without my groceries," I add, gesturing to the brown paper bag where I left it. Giving no further explanation, I reluctantly release Mary, take out my wallet, and grab a few twenties to toss on the counter. "My daughter ran off," I explain to security. Thankfully, he seems more understanding than the kid.

The same man who spoke up when they first arrived nods. "Ahh, I have two myself. All sorted." He smiles when his coworker passes me my change.

"All sorted," I agree, curling my fingers around the few notes and coins. The cashier nods toward a tip jar at the edge of his counter.

He's fucking joking, right?

I give him a look that says just that and shove my fist into my pants pocket, tucking away my change.

"Hand please, Piglet. Little girls who rush off don't get to roam freely," I remind her. With the bag secured in my left arm, I offer Mary my right.

Security chuckles at the pout she gives me. Their hushed words reach me as we turn to leave.

"Don't press that security button again unless you actually need security. Last warning."

With Mary's hand in mine, I scan the crowd as we head out, but I can't see the couple anywhere. The grip on my chest loosens more and more the closer we get to the exit. That is until the one person in the world determined to give me a heart attack decides that today is the day that I have it.

Bored with just holding my hand, Mary starts bouncing her rubber ball. Catching it clumsily, she bounces it again and again. The exit is only a few steps away when she pitches it a little too hard, the angle all wrong, and instead of coming back up to her, the ball scampers off. Bouncing right out of the building.

A jostle to my shoulder from someone entering through the exit door is all it takes. One minute I'm holding my daughter's hand, the anxiety is leaving my body, and the next, Mary is rushing after her damn ball, squeezing through the small cracks in the crowd like only a small child can.

Panicked, I try to follow, but there are just too many people.

"Mary!"

A tight fist closes over my heart, and I can't breathe.

"Mary!"

I shove through the crowd, people huffing as I push them out of the way. Then I hear it . . . a small scream of pain, followed by my daughter's cries.

I'm going to kill someone. Whoever it is, is a dead man.

I'm gasping, unable to breathe by the time I lay eyes on my sweet girl. Sitting on the cold floor, Mary hiccups, her tears not stopping. Blood rushes to my ears as I run the short distance that separates us.

A woman is crouched in front of my daughter. Okay, so I'm killing a woman today. *Won't be the first.*

Barely a few steps away now, the woman's words hit me. "Shhh, that's okay, sweetie. It's just a scrape." Her voice is sweet and calm, with a husk that sends a shiver running down my back.

Mary sniffles, and they both lean in, wanting a better look at Mary's bent leg. My eyes follow theirs. My daughter's flowery denim overalls have a large tear. Her knee is grazed, and it looks sore, with blood trickling from the wound.

My heart gives another sharp squeeze.

"Mary Lou!" I snap, my worry escaping as anger

and frustration. Both girls jump, and two sets of startled, wide eyes snap to me—one brown, one blue. One terrified, one guilty.

The woman shuffles closer to Mary. As if I'm not standing above them furious, Mary gives her new friend a small smile and then looks at her knee again. The woman, however, remains tense. Her brown eyes might be back on Mary and her head tucked down, but I see how she turns her ear toward me when I take a final step.

She's ready to fight . . . for a child she just met.

Raising an eyebrow, I stay silent, swallowing the urge to apologize. Since when the fuck do I do that? Especially when I've done nothing wrong.

Mary ran off, and this woman hurt her, I remind myself. *But I don't want them to be afraid.*

"Mary Lou," I repeat, much calmer.

Shoulders hunched, Mary finally turns to look up at me.

"I'm sorry, Daddy." And she is. Her words are quiet but sincere.

Anxiety slowly seeps from my body. Red catches my attention from the corner of my eye— blood. Her little knee really does look sore, but the woman is right. It's just a scrape.

"It's my fault," the woman defends, jutting her chin out.

Another shiver courses through my body. Only this time, it's not her voice that causes it. She's beautiful. Her big brown eyes meet mine defiantly, the fear from just a moment ago nowhere in sight. That is until I take in the rest of her face.

Thick dark lashes surround her glaring eyes, her tan cheeks are flushed, and her cute nose flares as she breathes in deep, but what really gives her away is the death grip her teeth have on her bottom lip.

Yep, definitely having a heart attack today.

My heart isn't the only thing that's stirring. I'm getting a hard-on outside of the grocery store. Who the fuck is this woman?

Dropping down, I quickly join them on the ground. Startled, the woman flinches and falls on her ass.

"Careful," I warn, reaching out to steady her. A wide-eyed stare is my only answer, and we're back to terrified. My cock twitches, a smirk settling on my lips.

I turn my attention to Mary. "What did I say about running off?"

"Not to," my daughter mumbles.

"I ran into her," the woman rushes.

"Nuh-uh." Mary shakes her head. "I wasn't looking. I just wanted my ball."

At least one of them is being honest. "Lying is not tolerated in this family," I warn.

"But I'm not lying," Mary huffs with a little too much attitude from the person who caused this mess. I give her a look.

"I didn't mean you, Piglet." Turning to the woman who captured my attention with one look, I repeat, "Lying is not tolerated in this family."

Her slim throat bobs. "Yes, sir," she whispers so low I barely hear it.

"So try again," I tell her sharply, enjoying how her body shivers.

"I was told to be quick, so I rushed into the building just as . . ." She pauses for a second, "Mary Lou rushed out. It was both our fault." Her eyes flicker to Mary, whose face is scrunched up.

"Mary Lou is for when she's in trouble, which she is," I remind my daughter, then turn back to my brown-eyed girl. "Otherwise, it's just Mary," I explain.

"Or Piglet!" Mary adds.

"Or Piglet," I agree with a chuckle.

"Well, I like Piglet." The woman reaches out and gently wipes away my daughter's tears, which have thankfully stopped. "Is it because you wear pigtails?"

Mary frowns, her small hands holding one of her braids. "I don't know."

Both turn to me, looking for an answer, and something inside me shifts.

Never in Mary's life have I thought she needed a mother until now. This moment was meant to happen. The three of us are meant to happen.

"No, it's because she loves pigs. What's your name?" I ask, wanting to know exactly who my future wife is.

Her eyes flicker between mine before she finally answers, "Lulu. It's Louise, but my grammy used to call me Lulu, and it stuck."

Mary squeals, "Mine's Louise!"

"Mary Louise," I elaborate. "Louise was my mother's name."

"And we match!" Mary rushes, poking an embroidered flower on Lulu's denim overalls.

Lulu grins, not seeming the least bit perturbed by my daughter's enthusiasm. "I guess we do. Although yours are cooler since they have way more flowers than mine."

Mary's shoulders drop along with her excitement. "I ruined them."

"No, baby, it's just a tear. A needle and thread and they'll be as good as new. Maybe your mommy could even sew a flower over to hide it."

I cringe internally at Lulu's words. Opening my mouth, I go to correct her, but my daughter beats me to it.

"I don't have a mommy. She's in heaven," Mary whispers, shredding my heart.

"Oh."

A blanket of silence settles over us, awkward and sad.

"I don't have a daddy. He's in heaven too," Lulu whispers, her words not traveling outside our small triangle.

Mary blinks quickly, her eyes searching when she looks at Lulu. "Do you think they're together?" she asks, turning toward me.

I frown at the question. She's never asked anything like this before . . . We rarely mention her birth mother.

"Maybe," I answer, stroking my hand over the back of her head.

"So Mommy's not lonely without us?"

My heart squeezes. Mary will never know what truly happened to her mother . . . or her birth father.

A ball of emotion lodges in my throat, cutting off any words I could come up with.

"Yeah, baby, I think they're together." Lulu nods, answering for me as she blinks back tears.

Piglet's head bobs along with ours. With my left hand, I wipe her small cheek, and reaching out her right hand, Lulu wipes Mary's other cheek until we're both happy my daughter's tears are gone.

Sneaking a look at me, Lulu gives a small, sad smile.

Fuck, I'm in trouble . . . and so is she.

CHAPTER TWO

Lulu

My heart is breaking. How can the world be so unfair?

Mary glances back down at her knee, dry-eyed and calmer, but pain still spears my chest. Every little girl should have their mother, but at least she has her dad. His large hand moves from her cheek to cup the back of her head.

I miss my dad. My chin trembles, and my throat closes.

Blinking quickly, I blow out a heavy breath. It's been fourteen years, and I'm still waiting for it to get easier. I was only a couple of years older than Mary, and life just never got better.

I jump when strong fingers brush against my cheek. I hadn't realized I was crying. My face heats, and the tips of our fingers brush when I roughly wipe my tears away with the back of my hand. With a sniffle, I turn away from him.

The same strong fingers that were so gentle just a second ago grip my chin tightly, forcing my gaze back to his, where he holds it hostage.

"Ajax," he breathes.

I frown, my eyes dropping to his lips.

"My name," he elaborates.

My face warms again.

"Daddy, can I have ice cream because I hurt my knee?"

Ajax's lip spread wide. I hadn't thought he could get any more handsome, but I was wrong. My body shivers in protest when he releases his hold on my chin.

"No, you had more than enough sugar last night. But you can have a Band-Aid with a pig on it."

The flash of disappointment on Mary's face instantly disappears. *She really does love pigs.* The three of us sit on the ground, all awkwardness and sadness gone, and for just a second, I feel normal. Just a small family out for the day, but the illusion doesn't last long.

"Ahh," I cry out, staggering to my feet.

A painful grip on my arm is unrelenting, the owner uncaring if I fall. Ajax is on his feet before I am, Mary hidden behind him as he moves to shield her. Something flashes across his face, something dark and cruel. It's gone just as quickly as it came, but I saw it, and I recognize it. It's a look I've seen before . . . often.

When Andrew gets mad. It's as if something takes over him, or maybe that's when the real Andrew comes out. Either way, it's never good when I see it.

My chest heaves but not in fear of Ajax. I'm not scared of him. I know I should be since I saw what he's hiding, but I'm not.

Stumbling, I manage to catch myself on wobbly legs.

"Daddy," Mary calls out. She's as terrified as I am at the sudden attack.

Steady, I turn my head only to see my mother's husband, Andrew, standing there, a sneer twisting his face.

"I told you to be quick. Go get in the fucking car."

He shakes me roughly, shoving me toward the parking lot hard enough that I trip down the first step.

I twist, looking back to try to see Mary. I can't leave her like this. Her frightened cries are shredding my heart. I need to show her I'm okay, but Ajax has shifted with us, moving so that his tall body continues to shield her.

He's a good dad, and my heart pulls again. The sight of Ajax protecting his daughter eases me slightly. No one is hurting her, not while he's around.

"It's okay, Mary." My voice is cheery, hopefully enough to fool her. "I'm sorry," I mouth to Ajax. He doesn't respond; he just stands there with his strong arms crossed over his chest. A wall of strength.

A breath shudders into my chest. I need to leave before I start crying on the steps of the grocery store. Humiliation rolls through me. I hate that they saw this, but they're not the first, and they won't be the last.

Quickly, I turn away. I can't stand to see Ajax's blank stare anymore.

"Did you even go into the damn store? Fucking useless," Andrew hisses, his foot connecting with the back of my knee.

My leg buckles, forcing me to rush down a few steps clumsily, but I don't fall.

I shouldn't stop again. I know better, but Andrew's already mad, and I can't help myself, so fuck it.

Huffing one last deep breath, I try to calm myself and turn. I meet Ajax's gaze, but my eyes drop away quickly.

Mary peeks around her dad's legs, having stood up. Her small hands cling to him like a lifeline. Lifting my hand, I give her a short wave.

"Bye, baby," I whisper.

A small wave back is the only answer I get.

My shoulders drop as I turn and walk away, my mother's husband no more than a step behind me the entire time. His hand clips the back of my head when we reach his car.

"All you had to do was go get fucking groceries."

Andrew Clarke may be the man whose surname I carry, but he is not my father.

My mom watches from inside the car without a

word. I know better than to say anything. Why bother when she'll just take his side?

Try not to upset him, Lulu. It's your fault he's mad, Lulu. Just behave, Lulu.

Swallowing, I slide into the back seat, wrapping my arms around my stomach.

"And don't think you're sleeping in the house tonight," Andrew warns, looking back at me through the rearview mirror.

At twenty-one, this is all I have. A stepfather who hates me, a mother who stays quiet, and a tent to sleep in when I'm locked out.

How sad is that?

CHAPTER THREE

Ajax

My body hums, every nerve ending awake and ready.

Ready to kill, ready to take.

Only once before have I felt this pull with another person, that feeling of family, of them belonging with me, to me. Mary. I knew the minute that I saw her mother, pregnant and begging for the life of her unborn child, that the infant she carried was meant to be my baby. No one would care for or protect it like I could.

Images of the past add to the thrill that the idea of growing our family gives me.

My muscles are locked. It took every ounce of control that I had not to react when he grabbed Lulu. The grimace and pain on her pretty face were enough to kill me. But yelling, fighting, or reacting would have only gained attention and made the moment memorable for those around us.

Not what we want . . . not when that asshole's about to go missing.

"Daddy," Mary mutters, bringing my attention back to her.

I hate the look of fear on her face.

"It'll be okay, princess," I say, kissing the side of her head.

I scoop her up and settle her on my hip. I dread the day that my little girl gets too big to carry, but maybe by then, Lulu will have given her a sibling . . . or five, if I have anything to say about it.

The thought of Lulu round and full with my child sets something off inside me like a switch being flicked.

Lulu will be pregnant by the time I get her to her new home in Wisconsin, whether she likes it or not.

Mary moves, leaning down to look at her knee, which is no longer bleeding.

"Daddy'll fix it," I reassure.

Mary frowns but doesn't say anything. Maybe it's not just her knee bothering her.

"You never have to be afraid while I'm here," I remind her.

"He scared me," she whispers, wrapping her small arm around my neck.

I shift her so she can cuddle in close but stay silent, giving her time to gather her feelings.

Finally, my sweet girl whispers, "He hurt Lulu."

"I know." I nod. "Daddy'll fix that too."

She blinks at me, not quite understanding the meaning beneath my words, but that's okay. She will when she wakes up, and Lulu is in the RV traveling on the road with us.

Still standing at the top of the stairs near the entrance, I watch Lulu and the asshole who manhandled her walk between the parked cars and stop near a shitty-looking Ford.

That motherfucker just hit her! Fuck going missing. Everyone's going to see what I do to him. *I'm going to display him like a fucking trophy!*

Lulu is crying as she climbs into the back of the car. The man walks around to the driver's side door, a smirk plastered on his face. My lips twitch. He has no idea what's coming for him.

Something tickles at the back of my mind, an instinct that's kept me alive and free until now. Trusting that part of my brain, I skim my gaze across the top of the cars.

That's when I see him.

How the fuck had I forgotten?

I was so wrapped up in a woman for the first time in my life that everything else had melted away. Including the knowledge that another killer is in the same vicinity. *Fuck!*

I am better than that. A better hunter, a better killer, and a better dad.

My arm tightens around my baby.

She's safe.

Scowling under my cap, I watch as the man from the store walks his cart back, his woman nowhere in sight. She's probably tucked safely inside their car.

At least one of us isn't acting like a complete fucking novice.

My eyes stay with him, unsure of what he has in mind. I've never met someone else with the same . . . proclivities as me, not that we go around announcing ourselves.

This is a day of firsts for me. Finding my woman and a fellow hunter in the same town, at the same place. What are the chances?

His eyes stay rooted on me, clearly just as cautious.

We need to get out of Cromwell quickly—with Lulu and without setting off any alarm bells. But most of all, we need to leave without pissing off the locals.

Fighting every instinct I have, I take my eyes off him for a fraction of a second, just long enough to look at Lulu, where she still sits crying in the back of the car, and then back to the man from the store.

He follows my gaze and frowns.

Without any other way of asking, I look toward the car again, pinning the two in the front with a look that hopefully shows my hatred. Not a second later, I watch as understanding washes over his face.

A slight, discreet nod gives me all the permission I need. But he's not finished. He returns his gaze to the car, looks at Lulu, and shakes his head. It's barely noticeable, but I see it. And it boils my blood. She's not his to deny!

Does he think that he has a claim to her? Does he know her? Is she family? It doesn't matter. None of it does. I was asking out of respect, a courtesy.

Lulu is mine. No matter who tries to get between us, I'm taking her with me. A smile spreads over my face.

She may not know it yet, but Lulu's taken and coming home with us.

CHAPTER FOUR

Lulu

"Sally, where's the fucking food? I won't ask again."

The angry yell from the other room makes me jump. My head snaps up, and I lock gazes with my mom's panicked eyes. For a fraction of a second, we're on the same page. A team of just the two of us against my impatient stepdad.

But it doesn't last for long. It never does.

I always end up alone.

"You heard him. Give me his food," she snaps.

Scooping up more chicken and gravy out of the steaming pot, I pour it over the biscuits on his plate, and the smell makes my mouth water.

A thump sounds out from the living room.

"You couldn't just go into the store yesterday and get what he wanted, could you? You knew we wouldn't have time today. He wanted steak, so now he's going to spend the night angry," my mom snaps.

Forcing out a breath, I try to calm my nerves. Arguing with her won't do any good, and neither will reminding her that Andrew is always angry.

Living here never gets easier.

Beer sloshes in the bottle the closer we get. Tonight's going to be bad. I can feel it.

Andrew is on the sofa watching an old football game with his table tray waiting in front of him.

My mom sets his food down first, and his beer follows. I step away quickly.

Maybe it won't be so bad?

A loud crash proves me wrong.

"Ahh," Mom and I scream together, jumping back.

Open-mouthed, I take in the mess. He's thrown the whole table, food and all, across the room. Chicken and vegetables drip down the wall, and shards of plate litter the carpet.

"It's fucking cold!" he roars.

"It just cooked," I argue, barely above a whisper, but it was loud enough.

Andrew's head snaps around to where we both stand. Mom slaps a hand over her mouth as if to show it wasn't her.

"What did you just say?" he growls.

"It just cooked," I repeat shakily but louder.

His face shifts. *There's that look again.*

26

I know what's coming, so I do the only thing I can. Run.

Turning, I make a break for the back door. I just need to make it through the kitchen. Dropping low as I pass the front door, I snatch up my large gym bag that I'd previously stashed for easy access and keep moving. Every second counts. At five-eleven, Andrew is bigger and stronger than me but not quicker.

My heart pounds, punching to get out of my chest. I'm almost there.

Panting, I grab at the bowl of biscuits managing to clutch two just as the bowl slips off the side. I shove them in my mouth as I rush the last few steps, twist the lock, and slide the back door open.

Cold air hits my face and bare arms but the sound of ceramic crunching under heavy feet propels me forward into the dark yard.

Light from the house shines over the path, but that means he can see me too.

Pulling the biscuits out of my mouth, I gasp for more air.

"Fucking bitch! Someone needs to teach you a fucking lesson," Andrew screams after me.

Crossing over into the tree line, I don't look back.

Twigs, leaves, and debris crack under my sneakers. I don't think I've ever been more grateful for always having cold feet. It's the reason I wear shoes in the house.

I keep running, pushing my body forward until all house lights are gone, no one is nearby, and the only thing illuminating the forest around me is the night sky.

As soon as my feet slow, the adrenaline hits me differently. My body shakes. Fear and shock entwine, then flow through my body.

A sob rips out of my chest.

I can't keep doing this. Something needs to change.

Shame and humiliation consume me, and my body crumples. It's one thing for people to suspect that Andrew knocks my mom and me around, but it's another thing for them to know I sleep outside to avoid his fists.

At least I got my bag.

I shiver, remembering the first night he chased me out of the house. No coat, no blanket, no shelter, no hope. That had been a long fucking night, one I'd learned from. The small pop-up tent in my bag wouldn't do much in a bear attack, but as far as rain and wind go . . . it'll do.

For a second, I think about staying at Cromwell's summer camp. The grounds are closed for winter, so it'd be safe. But after the Halloween party some college kids threw, the cabins will be locked up like Fort Knox.

Besides, Sam Cromwell might be my friend, but I still don't want to risk pissing off her brothers.

I heave a sigh, shuffle to my knees, and tug the bag closer. Might as well get comfy for the night.

CHAPTER FIVE

Ajax

"Piglet, that's three stories. We agreed on two," I remind Mary with a raised brow.

A cheeky smile is my only answer, followed by a small pout.

"Mary," I stress.

My daughter sighs, resigned.

"One more?"

Now, I'm sighing. Settling back against the headboard, I ignore her grin of triumph. One day, I'll stop being a pushover.

One day, she'll stop asking me to read her a bedtime story, I remind myself. Might as well enjoy it while I can. She won't be a baby forever, even if she'll always be my baby. So I read her a fourth story, a fifth, and a sixth.

Safe in the knowledge that she's fast asleep, I make

my way out of her small room, quietly closing the door. Once asleep, that girl won't wake up for nothing short of a bomb.

My eyes scan the windows even though I know they're locked. Mary will be safe while I'm out.

We're parked in the town's RV park. While not busy enough that I'm worried about being seen, it is populated enough that a break-in is not happening. Not that anyone is getting past the four locks on our motorhome.

The idea of leaving her here eats at me, but it can't be avoided. A babysitter would highlight that I'm not here, taking my alibi if I need it. Besides, experience tells me the guy from the grocery store will be with his girl tonight, the same as last night. He wants to keep his distance the same as I do. I don't know what it is, but my gut tells me Mary is safe here while I'm out. If I thought otherwise, I wouldn't leave.

Not for anything or anyone.

Walking through the RV, I pick up my quiver and bow, thumbing the bowstring.

My blood heats. I can't remember ever being this excited for a hunt. The anticipation has been killing me since yesterday.

My plan of snatching her away last night was killed quickly when a camper farther down decided that a late Halloween party was in order. Fucker and his friends were outside drinking until three in the morning, forcing me to wait until tonight. Even tracking that shitty Ford to her house hadn't helped ease my needs.

At least Mary had slept through the music. But the air outside tonight is cold and still. Everyone on the site is tucked away in their motor homes.

My cock twitches, growing.

Tonight is different. I'm not just hunting for the kill. Today, I'm bringing home a trophy.

A smirk pulls at the corner of my mouth.

Time to go hunting.

CHAPTER SIX

Lulu

My breathing is obnoxiously loud in the small tent, or maybe I'm just being paranoid. My ears practically twitch at every sound outside the flimsy walls. It's never nice on nights I have to run, but today feels different.

Another sound makes me sit up, and the thin sleeping bag falls, bunching at my hips. Goose bumps pop up and spread down my bare arms.

Definitely need to remember a sweater next time. Sleeping in the forest in a tank top is just not it. My leggings aren't much better.

Relax, I remind myself, *it's just the wind.*

I start to lower myself back when I hear it again.

It's not the wind. *Fuck.*

Why couldn't I just tell Sam what's happening? The Cromwells would take me in. *Stupid pride.*

Tears fill my eyes. The sound is getting closer.

A voice calls out, and even though I can't make out the words, I know it's him. Running wasn't enough this time. Andrew's come for me.

His mocking tone taunts me.

Fear punches me in my throat.

What the fuck am I supposed to do? There's no one out here. That was the point. No one to stumble upon, no one to help me.

I crawl forward, but my hand hesitates above the zipper.

Stay or run.

My mind screams at me to pick one.

"I'm going to teach you a fucking lesson, you little bitch," Andrew threatens. His voice is clear, so he's close.

Spying my sneakers in the corner, I make a decision.

I'm not waiting for him to find me. I can't best him in a fight, but I can outrun him.

Slipping my shoes on quickly, I curse myself again for forgetting a jacket. I take a deep breath and then another.

Now or never.

Don't stop.

CHAPTER SEVEN

Ajax

The house is brightly lit, illuminating the backyard and making me cringe. I keep close to the wall that leads to the back door. There's no camera, but I don't want any residents to glance out and see me sneaking inside.

Even dressed in camouflage and a ski mask, there's no hiding from this light. It's coming from every fucking room. It's the middle of the night. They're supposed to be in bed like the rest of the town.

Reaching out my right arm, I grip the door handle while staying plastered to the wall. With one hard shove, the door slides on the track.

It's unlocked.

A grin takes over my face, even as a stab of disappointment hits my chest. I was hoping for a good hunt tonight, but they're making it easy.

Their house doesn't have a close neighbor on either side. It's run down and set back off a side road, so getting into the backyard unseen wasn't hard. A fucking amateur could get in here undetected.

Anger returns. That motherfucker is the man of the house. He's supposed to make sure Lulu is safe and that the house is locked up tight at night.

After his performance at the grocery store, I shouldn't be surprised, but I am. Surprised and disgusted.

Some men don't deserve their families, but it's okay because I'm about to take his.

A satisfied thrill settles in my bones. Maybe tonight will be fun after all.

The kitchen is a mess. Food, glass, and ceramic litter the floor. The shards crunch under my feet, making my jaw twitch.

So much for entering unnoticed.

I still, listening for movement farther in the house, but the only sound that reaches me is my own breathing.

Hopefully, they're all asleep. By the mess, I assume they've worn themselves out.

Carefully but quickly, I get it over with, crossing the room as fast as possible. I scrub my boots on the carpet when I step off the tiled floor, knocking loose anything stuck in the soles.

The kitchen leads me to a small entryway with

coats and shoes neatly piled and hooked by the front door. The stairs to my left tease me, but I need to clear the bottom floor first. There is nothing worse than being caught unaware.

For all I know, the useless bastard might have fallen asleep on the couch. The room is empty, and nothing is worth noting except a small overturned table and a mess of discarded food. Looks like someone lost his temper.

My excitement turns to worry at the mess. Lulu had better be sleeping safely in her room; otherwise, someone would be dying slowly tonight.

Dread seeps into my bones. Something is off. Even in a house like this, something is not right.

Silently, my feet carry me upstairs. The second floor is small, with just three doors. I push open the only door that isn't completely closed. The bathroom is empty and dark.

My heart pounds.

Pressing my ear to the next door, I strain, but nothing greets me. Backing away, I do the same with the last door, frowning when the same nothingness greets me.

It's impossible to know who is behind each door and where the danger lies. This is why I prefer hunting outside. There's nowhere for people to hide.

Fuck it. Left it is.

My hand closes around the doorknob, twisting slowly and without a sound. Just like the rest of the house, the bedroom light is on, making it easy to see the prone body lying on the bed. She's the woman from earlier, who was in the front seat of the car.

Her dad is gone, but maybe this is her mom? It doesn't matter; she let that prick touch my girl, and that can't go unpunished.

An open bottle of wine sits three-quarters empty on the bedside table next to where she's passed out. The man from the store is nowhere in sight. The dread from earlier returns.

Backing out of the room, I head to the other, reaching it in seconds. This house really is small—not that I can talk with the RV, but Lulu will have more room once we're back at my cabin. *Our cabin,* I correct myself.

I hesitate outside of what can only be Lulu's room, my gut churning.

A sigh escapes me, the doorknob heavy in my hand. Empty.

Where the fuck is my girl?

Backing out of the dark room, I remove my knife from the sheath at my lower back. The weight in my hand, comforting. The drop point blade catches the light, making my cock stir. Yeah, tonight will definitely be fun.

Time to get some answers.

The woman on the bed hasn't stirred, her frame exactly where I left her. I eye the bottle on the bedside. Although fun, tonight may not be as easy as I expected.

Sitting on the bed, I shuffle closer, my head tilting

as I watch her sleep. She looks peaceful . . . I can fix that.

Not needing it just yet, I tuck my knife away.

My large palm clamps down on her mouth, my thumb and forefinger pinching her nose closed. Let's wake her up. I reach over with my other hand, grab the abandoned wine, and pour it over her face.

Warm red wine trickles down the back of my gloved hand. The woman beneath my hold starts to shake her head—slowly at first, then frantic. She struggles, her hands shoving and hitting out at my chest. Her movements are sloppy. She's drunk, and I'm bigger. This won't end well for her, and she knows it.

"Do I have your attention?"

When she doesn't respond, I repeat myself.

"Do I have your attention?"

Her head bobs.

"Good. You will answer my questions quickly and quietly. If anything other than that leaves your mouth, my hand returns to where it is now. A third time and I will not lift my hand until you stop breathing. Am I understood?"

She nods frantically, her watery eyes bulging.

Good.

"Lulu, where is she?"

I lift my hand slowly, hovering it over her mouth.

"I don't know," she rushes.

"Are you her mother?" *How angry will my girl be when I kill her?*

Sneering, the woman on the bed nods.

No love lost there, then. I raise a brow at her silent answer. How did Lulu come from this and still be so caring and sweet to a strange child?

"The man at the store, who is he?"

"My husband. Please don't hurt us. You can take what you want," she cries.

Some people just have to learn the hard way. I roll my eyes.

My hand clamps down, my thumb and forefinger gripping her nose again.

Now, it's my turn to sneer.

Satisfaction and arousal course through me as she struggles. Her fingers clutch at my covered shoulders, her eyes pleading.

Only when I know that her lungs are burning do I let go.

"I ask questions; you answer. That's it," I snap.

Too busy gasping, she doesn't respond.

"Where is Lulu?" I try again.

"I don't know. The bitch ran off again," she sobs between gulping breaths.

My body tenses at her words.

"What the fuck happened downstairs?"

I'm shaking with anger before I even have my answer.

"She made Andrew mad. Can't even cook him dinner right."

"Is she hurt?"

I brace for the answer.

"I don't know." I believe her.

"Where is your husband?"

My chest gets tighter the longer she remains silent.

"I don't know," she whispers.

My chest relaxes.

"But he's with her."

Her words make my world stop. My eyes move up, searching her gaze. She's scared, yes, but something else is hidden beneath. Whatever that asshole is doing to my girl, her mother wants it to happen.

My hand closes around her neck instinctively.

"Where would Lulu run?"

Her mother shakes her head.

Not good enough.

"Where?" I hiss.

The sound that leaves her is inhuman. That of a woman desperate to live. My hold loosens enough to let her words slip out.

"The woods. She ran out back," she coughs out.

Seems I do get to go hunting tonight after all.

"He followed?"

She nods as best she can with the viselike grip I have on her neck.

"Is he armed?"

She shakes her head.

"You said Lulu's run before. Does he always follow?"

Another negative head motion.

Good, that means she has an advantage. He doesn't know where she runs to.

But it means this time is different. If he catches her . . .

I shove away the awful thought. I need to leave. Now.

"Then it seems we're done here." I give a small nod.

The hand twisting in my jacket relaxes a little.

"You should have protected her. That's a parent's job. Now, you're just as bad as he is." My hand moves up to clamp her mouth again. I need her neck clear for what's coming next.

Fortunately for her, I'm out of both time and patience. I need to find my girl before her stepfather does something. Reaching behind me, I grip the hilt of my knife. Now, she's truly panicking.

As she should.

Using the hold on her face, I tilt her head back slightly, pushing her farther into the pillow.

The curved edge of the blade makes quick work of cutting through the skin of her throat. The slice is clean and precise.

Blood spills out, soaking her shirt. The bright lights of the room make the red so much more thrilling.

Life seeps out of her onto the rumpled bedsheets. But my usual calmness is nowhere to be found. My body remains tense and wound up.

I need to find my girl.

First, I'm going to save her, and then, I will take her.

CHAPTER EIGHT

Lulu

I unzip the tent just enough to crawl out on my hands and knees. Hopefully, he wastes enough time stopping to look in here so I can make it out of the forest without ending up in his crosshairs.

Frigid air slaps me in the face as soon as I'm exposed. It's so much worse out here. I guess the tent hadn't been so useless after all.

Pushing to my feet, I take off to the left. Hard and fast, I push myself more than ever.

Andrew has never come looking for me before. He's usually too drunk and lazy to bother. Everything about tonight has been different. His fuse is short and explosive, but this is something else.

My stomach churns when I think about why he's out here.

Clouds of cold air puff out of me as I pant. My palm scrapes against the tree bark, but the boost it gives when I push off them is well worth the pain. I change direction, shoving off another tree.

"Little fucking bitch," he roars through the forest, followed by sounds of crashing.

He found the empty tent.

It won't take him long to figure out where I went.

My chest screams, the freezing air burning as I suck it in quicker.

This is the last time. I have to leave. I can't stay anymore, even if it means being alone.

Being drunk hasn't slowed him down too much. Andrew covers the ground between us quickly.

Threats of what he will do when he catches me make my steps falter in fear.

I'd rather die.

My rushed feet snap the twigs loudly, but speed is more important right now. It's not like I can hide. He'd find me.

His feet are heavy, and his stride is much longer than mine. *Where is he?*

Twisting my neck, I try to glance behind me.

Big mistake.

Something on the ground catches my foot, making me stumble. I try to catch my balance but stagger clumsily.

Just as my feet steady, something big and heavy slams into me, knocking the wind out of me and taking me to the ground.

We land with a thud.

Pain courses up my side.

Fuck.

Large hands shove my shoulder until I'm on my back, then wrap around my throat and squeeze.

Andrew moves above me, his knees on either side of my body, his weight overwhelming as he sits on me.

My vision blurs. His sneering face looms above me.

"I told you I'd catch you," he taunts.

The smell of alcohol on his breath churns my stomach.

My hands shove at his chest but do nothing to move him. Balling them, I punch wildly.

I don't want to die in the forest.

My vision becomes worse. Tears build, and I can barely see.

"Lulu!"

Did someone call my name? *No.* No one knows I'm out here.

This is it. This is how it ends for me.

I turn my eyes away, not wanting his face to be the last thing I see. My tears spill out, dropping onto the cold forest floor.

Movement behind Andrew makes my heart jump with hope. Someone had screamed my name.

Someone has come for me!

My gaze flicks back to Andrew. He's oblivious to the fact that someone is here. Am I so far gone that I'm hallucinating? One last hope of living?

The figure moves quickly. Their hands are steady and confident when gripping the back of my stepfather.

Andrew is ripped off me, his hands pulling my neck up with him. My body flops back down roughly while coughs consume me. My lungs scream for air.

My chest expands over and over. Breaths shuddering in and out.

Andrew curses, making threats, but it holds little weight when he's being thrown into a tree like a rag doll.

Shoving himself off the bark, Andrew uses his weight to move my savior. They stumble backward together.

My coughing stops while the two fight.

Andrew goes down onto the forest floor quickly. He's drunk, and the other man is both stronger and quicker.

The two men grapple next to me. My mystery man pins my stepfather's body beneath him. A hand on the back of Andrew's head shoves him into the ground.

Eat dirt.

The unknown man's head snaps to me so fast I wonder if I spoke aloud. Even this close, I struggle to recognize him. But I must know him since he knew my name.

Green and black paint covers his face, along with the shadows of the forest. His head tilts, our eyes locking. His lips spread in a menacing smile, and his white teeth peek through. He looks like a predator about to get his prey.

Then he opens his mouth, and my whole world stops for the third time tonight.

"Run," he growls.

Blinking, I lie beside them as Andrew struggles to break free.

He looks down at my tormentor beneath him with disgust, then back at me.

Is he going to release Andrew?

Time slows as our eyes lock again.

"Run," he roars, startling me.

The word echoes, bouncing from tree to tree.

I roll onto my stomach and scramble to my feet. Fear, terror, and hatred return double fold. Most of all, I feel anger. I thought he was here to help. I thought he cared and would save me.

Turning my head, I spit, "Fuck you." Not waiting for a response, I run.

CHAPTER NINE

Ajax

My brows shoot up at her words, and a chuckle escapes me.

Little shit.

The piece of crap beneath me takes advantage of my distraction.

Shooting his elbow back, he connects with the side of my head hard enough to tilt me backward and loosen the grip I have on his head.

Well, that achieved nothing.

I'm still on his back. All he's done is piss me off more. I was going to release him anyway. *Dickhead.*

My girl knew that, and that's why she's mad. She knows what's coming.

Kind of, I smirk.

This piece of shit's not getting anywhere near her

again. The only one who touches her from now on is me.

Glancing up, I see Lulu running through the trees. She's pushing herself, and the distance between us is almost too much to bear.

After tonight, I'll always be close, and on the few occasions that I'm not, she'll be bound and gagged, waiting for me to come home. Until I can trust her not to run, she'll never have a moment's peace. I'll own her—mind, body, and soul.

Every part of her being will crave me. She won't want me to leave. More importantly, she won't want to leave.

Lulu will be mine, just as much as I am hers. She doesn't know it yet, but this woman owns me. I'll do anything for her, and anything to keep her . . . which she's about to find out.

This is going to be fun, my best kill yet. I smirk.

CHAPTER TEN

Lulu

I can't help it. It's like my body has a mind of its own as I twist and glance back. I should have learned the first time that nothing good comes from looking back.

It got me caught last time, and as I watch my camouflaged man release Andrew, I can't help but think it's going to do the same this time too.

My feet skid to a stop.

I knew it, asshole!

Tears fill my eyes.

Are all men jackasses? *No, the Cromwells are good men.*

Why save me if he's just going to watch Andrew chase me down in the end?

My stepfather lies still for a second, shocked that he's being released. He looks back at the other man, then straight at me. His face screws into an ugly sneer.

My breath catches in my throat.

How can people be so evil?

I need to get to Sam's house. Hopefully, her dad is home. *Fuck,* should I go to their cabin? Their home in town is closer, *if I can make it.*

Andrew is on his feet. He gives one last look behind him, then takes a step forward. Every move brings him closer to me.

I'm frozen, standing unblinking as he closes the distance.

Run!

My body's not listening.

Movement behind the approaching man catches my attention.

What the . . . ?

His large form is crouched over a bag I hadn't noticed before. He starts taking things out. My brow furrows.

That's a fucking bow and arrow!

My stomach drops, and Andrew has nothing to do with it for once.

Run! my mind screams again. Spinning, I propel myself forward, and pure terror fuels me.

I run, my ears straining to hear what both men are doing, but all I can hear is Andrew. If I thought he was mad before, he's nuclear-level angry now.

He's catching up easily.

I hear something woosh through the air at the same time as I feel the breeze of Andrew's hand swing out and miss my hair by a fraction. He almost had me.

A roar of pain pierces the air. *Andrew!*

Stunned, I spin. My stepfather lies face down on the ground behind me, an arrow through his back. Pain is etched on his face as he peers up at me. Blood seeps out the corner of his mouth when he asks for my help.

I'm a statue, rooted in place.

The mystery man approaches, his walk calm and steady. My throat constricts. Less than a foot away from Andrew, he reaches behind, pulling out a large knife and taking my terror to a new level.

Who the fuck is he?

Fixated, I watch.

Our eyes meet, and his enjoyment is clear.

The knife plunges into Andrew's calf, and my stepfather's scream makes me jump. Our hunter smirks, his gaze returning to me.

Pulling the blade free, he sinks it into the body below him again and again. Each stab gets higher and higher until both he and I are panting.

Less than three feet apart. My feet are still planted where I stopped.

A hiccuped sound startles me. Reaching up, I find my cheeks wet. Andrew isn't the only one crying. But he's the only one begging.

I don't say a word. I don't plead for him or beg the stranger to stop. Instead, I continue to stand here.

Watching.

The man before me smiles. His hand wraps around the hilt, the blade sliding free of Andrew's lower back. Standing straight, his feet on either side of the writhing body on the forest floor, he surveys me.

His eyes wander, making me feel more exposed than the cold wind ever could. My skin is flushed despite my body shivering.

His right leg swings over Andrew, and he walks closer. Confidently, he approaches, the bloody knife dripping at his side. His left hand shoots out, gripping my chin, and his fingers are surprisingly gentle as he holds me still.

Forcing me to meet his eyes, he smiles, the dry paint making his white teeth pop more. He looks almost wolfish, ready to devour me.

My eyes drop to his lips at the thought. It only makes him smile harder.

Tilting my head back, he slams his mouth down onto mine. This time, his touch is anything but gentle. His fingertips are harsh, and his lips cruel. Teeth attack my bottom lip, punishing me when I refuse entrance. But my denial doesn't last long.

His tongue attacks my own. He takes charge, owning my mouth. My body isn't my own. It takes everything I have not to respond, but a small moan still escapes.

The kiss turns to small pecks, insistent and repetitive. Slowly, they trail across my cheek and down my neck.

The angle he holds me at is painful, but I make no move to stop him. My arms stay at my side, my fingers twitching. If I reach out, I know it'll be to pull him closer, not to push him away.

His taller frame hunches slightly, his lips still attacking my skin. He slows as he nears the base of my neck.

Pain rips through me, and my scream punctuates the air. His teeth latch on bruisingly tight. Painful and erotic.

My arms shoot up to push him away, my hands shove at the front of his body, but he's a wall of muscle. His abs ripple under my palms.

His teeth finally release me, and his head pulls back to look down at me. The grip on my chin lowers to my throat.

There's no hiding my reaction. My chest heaves, my breasts brushing him with every inhale. My beaded nipples stand out even in the dark, my bra doing nothing to hide my arousal.

At least he can't tell how wet I am.

His blue gaze roams me again, a smirk taking over his face.

Maybe he does know. I glare.

Shame fills me at my body's response. *What the fuck is wrong with me?*

My eyes drop to his straining cock, the bulge in his trousers obvious. My inner walls flutter with want.

We're both sick.

The hand on my neck tightens when I gulp. His thumb rubs back and forth, his gaze narrowing.

I shuffle when he steps back, my chest expanding with a loud breath.

"Stay," he demands, pointing at my feet.

But it's too late. Panic and disgust roll through me, and I need to leave, to get somewhere safe before I do something that can never be taken back. Like fucking the man who's killing my stepfather. *The man who saved me.*

I push that thought away because the night's not over yet. *What if I'm his next victim?*

My stomach roils, and my feet move of their own accord. My tired body protests as I run. My heart drops when I don't hear footsteps behind me, but before I can dwell on what that means, something shoots past me, embedding itself into the tree to my right.

My feet dig into the soil as I stop sharply. *Oh, hell no!*

I dart left.

Another arrow blocks my path. Running straight, I pray my hunter won't shoot me in the back.

He doesn't, but it couldn't get any closer. I feel the arrow as it passes me. I swear it flies through the loose strands of my hair. The thought is enough to jolt me forward and make me stumble. My knees land harshly, my hands barely breaking the fall.

My palms scream as they scrape across foliage.

Finally, I come to a stop. My heart is in my throat. Face down in the dirt, I pant, exhausted.

Then I hear it.

He's approaching.

I reach my arm out, my hand spread wide, grasping at the ground. Dirt fills under my nails as I claw my way along. At a snail's pace, I army crawl across the floor.

Just a little farther.

Come on.

But it's no good.

A final warning halts me, an arrow piercing the soil inches from my hand. Large hands grasp my waist, tighten, then drag me back until my ribs are between his feet.

"I told you to stay. Consider this your first lesson, Lulu." His sharp tone is familiar.

I frown. *Where do I know that voice from?* My eyes widen. *Ajax!*

My body comes alive again. I shiver, my nipples beading.

Oh my God.

His hand leaves my right side but returns to my body quickly. Painfully, his hand makes contact with my ass over and over.

"Ahh, stop!" I scream, trying to claw my way out from where he has me beneath him.

"Stop struggling and take your punishment," he orders.

He's relentless, striking the right side of my ass

repeatedly. My cheek is on fire. Loudly, I sob, pleading with him to stop, but it's as if he can't hear me. Then again, Andrew's pleas yielded nothing either.

Why would I be any different? I cry harder.

As his hand continues to rain down, I shout out the only thing I can. "I'm sorry, I'll stay." My whole body shakes with my uncontrollable crying.

Burying my face in my folded arms, I squeeze my words out, "I'm so sorry, Ajax. I won't move. I promise."

His blows stop. His breath chuckles out. "Good, you're a quick learner. That will go in your favor. I'm a harsh teacher, Lulu, but you will learn."

I nod.

After one last slap to my ass cheek, Ajax stands. I can feel him towering over me. He's waiting to see if I can keep my word.

I will.

My ass fucking hurts, and I saw what he did to Andrew. I don't want him to punish me again. I'll be good.

Satisfied, he walks away, his steps more hurried as he leaves me sobbing on the ground.

I lie here listening with my eyes squeezed closed. A voyeur to Andrew's death.

A thrill runs through me with every scream he releases. My breath catches as I anticipate the next attack on his battered and bleeding body.

I'm enjoying this. *I guess I'm evil too.*

Something settles deep inside my soul. Andrew

deserves this. After years of torture and walking on eggshells, who am I to intervene now that someone has decided to give him the punishment he's earned?

The shouts and cries change, and I can hear the blood gurgle in his throat as he struggles to stay alive. My stomach roils again, and I gag.

I'm not made for this. A chuckle reaches my ears, reminding me that the gorgeous man I met earlier today is made for this.

He enjoys it.

Fresh tears leak out, and my crying starts anew. Not because Andrew is about to die, but because I don't care. I'm not sad. I'm horny.

My body pulses, shivering for reasons that aren't the cold air.

Ajax is sick, and so am I.

One last pained cry resonates out, followed by a short gurgle.

He's gone. Years of beatings, harsh words, and threats remind me that I'm not crying for Andrew. Fuck him. No, this pain I feel, this dread and guilt, it's for what's to come. For what I want to happen.

Boots crunch on fallen leaves. Twigs snap louder the closer he gets, and my ears buzz as blood rushes through me. Excitement, anticipation, and fear. Is this it? Am I next?

His boots touch my feet.

I could not get any more tense. My eyes squeeze closed, waiting for the first blow.

But it doesn't come.

Instead, Ajax drops down. First one knee, then the other, until he straddles my calves. Strong hands touch my hips. His thumbs dig into my back while his long fingers push into the crease of my leg and the top of my thighs, pulling to make me shift. Forcefully, he moves me onto my hands and knees.

I frown.

Once I'm where he wants me, his gloved hands slide under my tank top. *They feel wet.* The thought and the smell of copper makes me gag. Heaving sends me forward.

Ajax quickly tugs me back, delivering a quick slap to my still sore ass.

His breathing is labored.

"And I'm glad you know it's me. It'll make this next bit easier."

I shiver at his growled words.

Murderous fingers grip the band of my leggings, quickly ripping them down over my hips to mid-thigh. Taking my panties with them, he leaves my privates exposed to him and the night air.

"Ahh," I cry out, shocked.

Reaching back, I search blindly for my waistband. Pushing up with my left hand, I try to straighten enough to plant my left foot on the ground.

I don't get far.

A hand tangles with the hair at the nape of my neck, shoving me back down onto all fours. I scream and thrash as Ajax attacks my bare ass with his palm. He doesn't stop until my left cheek blazes.

"Please," I sob.

"Please what, Lulu?" he asks, switching to my right side.

"Please stop," I hiccup.

"Woman, I haven't even started."

He attacks my right ass cheek relentlessly.

His stance widens, his knees shifting out just a little, and then a hand moves lower to grip my inner thigh, spreading my legs a little. Ajax chuckles as his forefinger reaches up higher on my thigh.

I screw my eyes shut, my face heating. He feels it, my wetness. My pussy leaks more at the thought of him knowing. I can try to escape, to fight him, but I can't hide how my body reacts. A bead of liquid runs down my sensitive skin, continuing over his finger.

A growl sounds out behind me.

"I'm going to show you who you belong to, Lulu. Then I'm going to get rid of any evidence you and I were ever out here before we go pack up your shit at the house and go home to our daughter."

What?

His thick, long cock shoves inside me. Pain and pleasure attack my body at once as he hammers in and out of my untried body.

Shocked by the intrusion and unprepared for the pain, I struggle to catch my breath.

"A virgin," he groans. "You were meant for me, Lulu. Just accept it. Accept me," he demands with a particularly harsh thrust. Embedding himself all the way inside.

My body stretches, gripping his shaft and begging him to stay.

Ajax stills, his hands squeezing and then releasing my hips. I feel full and overwhelmed. It's no longer my ass that's on fire. It's my whole body. Heat consumes me.

Sex has never been a priority for me. Between school and working to pay rent since I started high school, I haven't really given it much thought, but right here, right now, with Ajax buried deep, grinding into me from behind . . . I don't know how I made it to twenty-one and survived without it, without him.

"Please," I beg, a frustrated moan grumbling out of me. I need something, anything. I just need more.

The large man behind me chuckles, grinding in deep, his hips rough on my sore ass.

"That's my girl. By the time I'm done training you, you'll never want to leave. You'll think of nothing but our little family and making it bigger."

I gasp at his words, pushing my hips back.

Please move.

His words rattle around in my head. What the fuck have I gotten sucked into? Images of my stepfather pleading with a knife jammed into his back, his legs stabbed and bleeding, join Ajax's words.

My breath leaves me on a sob. This is so wrong. We are wrong, yet I still need more.

"Fuck me. Please," I beg, "just fuck me." Sobbing loudly, I barely hear his response.

"You like that idea, huh? Well, how about we start trying to build our family now? I'm going to stuff you so full of cum that there's no question of it taking root. Every minute of every day, you'll feel me dripping out of you. Your new life starts now, Louise Whitler."

Whitler? My world stops.

He withdraws slowly. My body screams where he split me open. I don't know what's more painful—my entrance, where the tip of him spears me, or deep inside, where my bruised walls ache.

I'm dying of fear and anticipation of what is to come if this is what a few minutes of harsh thrusts have me feeling.

A hitch in his breath and a twitch of his fingers is all the warning I get. Ajax plunges his whole shaft brutally into me. Our gasps mix. Mine filled with an unfamiliar pain, his with pleasure.

Hit after hit, our hips join, rocking my whole body.

My fingers bite into the soil, desperate for leverage. I'm completely at his mercy, something that he refuses to give.

His cock spears me, hitting the same spot deep inside, over and over. Each touch makes my body sing.

My pained cries turn to pleasure, but that bite never leaves.

Ajax trails his hands up to encase my ribs. The wet sensation and the night air hitting my exposed skin as my top moves up make me shiver. The material on his palms is rough against my sides.

The slap of our hips rings out, his movement never stopping. The pace is harsh and unforgiving.

He shoves my top higher and higher until his hands are under my breasts. One final shove and the cold air bites at my nipples. My tank top and bra are bunched uncomfortably at the top of my chest.

The urgency of his actions rips another moan from deep within me, his own joining when his hands envelop my breasts.

The smell of copper has gotten stronger the higher his hands reach. His right sleeve has smeared a thick trail of a sticky wet substance along my side, adding to what his hands left. The cotton is pressed against the front of my ribs, sandwiched between his forearm and my skin. I hear it squelch as the drenched fabric shifts back and forth as Ajax rocks our bodies to and fro. Something drips off his sleeve and runs down my body, leaving a trail behind it to dry. The sensation tickles, causing my legs and arms to quiver and my pussy to clench.

The knowledge of why I smell copper and the feel of the wetness drying along my skin make me gag again, and my body jolts forward. My arms collapse, dropping my shoulders to the ground.

My face barely touches the soil before strong hands steady me. The grip on my breasts tighten, lifting me.

His hips continue to piston, never ceasing. My

cunt squeezes hard as I gag again. This man killed someone. He took a life seconds before I begged him to take my virginity.

I spasm again, gripping his cock tighter and tighter.

Fuck, fuck, fuck.

I scramble to get my hands perched and lock my elbows.

His pace increases, the force cruel. Blow after blow, my body takes him, gripping him more each time, both desperate to keep him embedded and so close to release.

My tears start anew, my eyes screwed shut as pain and need become so tangled that I can't tell them apart.

It's too much.

He's too much.

The hand on my left breast squeezes and releases relentlessly, while his right hand is latched on my right shoulder, tugging me back onto his enormous stick. His hips thrust hard enough to launch me forward each time, only for his right hand to force me back and take him again.

"Take my fat cock, Lulu. Take me," he hisses.

The sound of skin slapping, wetness, moans, and groans are sent out into the woods with only the forest life to hear. Thankful that no one else can see us, my body finally gives in and falls.

My scream rings out.

An orgasm rips through me. It's violent and excessive, just like the man who caused it. Ajax doesn't stop. Even now, he refuses to give me a second of mercy. Instead, both of his hands drop to my hips, bruising in their hold.

My locked arms shake. My small breasts swing as he fucks me roughly. His grunts quicken.

He's close.

His knees shift, touching mine as they cage me, and his whole body tenses. His hips lose all rhythm, and his cock assaults my pussy frantically.

I jolt, unprepared for the wetness that fills me.

"Ahh," Ajax roars.

I expect his hips to stop, but he keeps pumping. More and more wetness fills me until it leaks out, some of it running down the inside of my thigh.

He groans again, his movements gradually slowing to a stop, his hip resting against my ass. His hands rub from the curve of my hips to the bottom of my ass and back. His thumbs dig into my cheeks as he smooths over them, somehow helping the deep ache I feel there. The pain from my earlier spanking is now tenfold from our hips connecting over and over.

Both of us pant, a puff of cold air collecting in front of my face. My inner walls continue to pulse, giving the odd ripple. *A mini orgasm*, I think. I whimper as another one courses through me.

Shivering, I become aware of the November night air again on my cooling body. I can feel the dry blood that is smeared all over me. It pulls at my skin the more I shiver.

What the fuck did I just do?

I could lie to myself and say that Ajax forced me, but we both know that's not true. Even now, as our bodies calm and he softens inside me, my tunnel continues to flutter around him, reminding us both that I more than wanted this.

I had begged.

I found pleasure in his murderous hands.

I came with my stepfather's blood on me.

Ajax was right. I was made for him.

CHAPTER ELEVEN

Ajax

Pulling out, I shiver. Even in the dark, seeing our essence seep out of her is easy. My cock twitches, staying at half-mast. Something tells me I'm always going to be hard around this woman.

The cold air bites at my oversensitive cock.

"Fuck," I curse.

Tonight hadn't gone the way that I thought it would. I expected to steal her away, take her right out of her bed while her old family lay lifeless and bloody a room over.

Instead, her stepfather lies ten feet away, his life force seeping into the soil while my cum oozes out of her freshly fucked body.

I meant what I said earlier. I hope our family

extension starts now. I frown as more of my goodness leaves her. *That just won't do.*

Gripping the base of my wet shaft, I use the broad head to gather my cum, then push the thick liquid back in with it. Her entrance splits for me, and I ignore Lulu's whimper. Gathering even more, I shove it back inside. The third time, I ram my cock in deep, pushing it as far inside her as I can.

My right hand anchors in the middle of her back, steadying me. My palm is sticky on her cold skin.

The heat of our sex is leaving. We need to pack up soon, but I'm reluctant to leave the warmth of her body. I want the imprint of my cock to be a permanent mark inside her and for my hands to become so familiar with her body that my mind has its own personal map, one that no one else will ever see or own.

Lulu's body is mine. Her begging, pleading, and the way she came proved it, and her sobbing now tells me she knows it too.

All that's left for me to do is break her spirit, and she'll officially be mine.

Mind, body, and soul.

CHAPTER TWELVE

Lulu

I don't know how long we've knelt here connected, but Ajax finally withdraws, making me cringe. I feel weird, both empty and full, like his cock is still inside.

Boots appear in front of me, mud covering the top of the black leather and the shin of his pants. Trailing my gaze up, I crane my neck.

His hands fiddle with the zipper on his pants before securing the button. He straightens his top and jacket, then holds out his hand.

I blink up at him.

"Stand," he orders, gesturing with his hand for me to take it.

In a state of shock, I give him my right hand, standing with his help. My body exposed. My face flames.

I don't know whether to be grateful for the fact that my bra and top are bunched so that it stops me from seeing my naked body as I glance down.

A finger knocks under my chin, raising my gaze.

"Fucking perfect."

I blush hard at his words. My nipples are hard points as the breeze attacks them. My ass still feels warm from his actions, my leggings and panties are still mid-thigh, and as another river of our joined juices leaves me, I fight the urge to cry.

There's no hiding from what we did.

Ajax smirks, his eyes following the trail on my inner thigh. Reaching out, he swipes it with his finger.

I didn't think my face could get any redder, but I was wrong.

His wet fingers stop in front of my blushing face. Frowning, I roll my lips in because that is not happening. But it's not my mouth he goes for.

Lifting it to his own, Ajax wraps his lips around it. The sound of him sucking it clean is loud. He wants me to hear.

"Mmm," he moans with a wicked smile, releasing his finger with a pop.

Wide-eyed and shocked, I watch stunned. His hand shoots out, his fingers I just watched now grip the nape of my neck, pulling me forward.

I barely blink before his mouth is on mine. His kiss is just as rough as the rest of his touches. His teeth biting, his tongue intruding, and his taste consuming.

Underneath everything him is something else . . .

a taste of us. The knowledge makes me moan and my body quiver. The cold night disappears once more. The heat of my face spreads, infecting the rest of my body.

His left hand cups my bare ass, causing me to jump.

Our tongues duel, but he's playing with me. Tilting my neck more, Ajax crowds closer, standing to his full height and towering over me. My hand reaches up, holding on tightly to his forearm. Hesitantly, I raise my right arm, cupping my hand around his bicep.

Ajax taps my ass three times as if to say, "That's right."

I feel small and fragile. Yet for the first time in my life, half naked and out in the woods, I feel safe.

How sad is that?

My chin quivers. My lips tremble under his, but he's not dissuaded, demanding that I respond to his advances. My tears join our kiss. After a few more strokes of his tongue, Ajax releases my mouth.

He ventures left, licking away my sadness and leaving a final kiss on my nose. My heart pauses at the gesture.

What the fuck is happening?

With one last tap to my ass, Ajax steps away. I reach down to pull my pants up, but a large hand on my elbow stills me.

Ajax shakes his head and uses his grasp to straighten me.

"Stay, right here," he orders, pointing at the ground.

I frown but nod. I learned that lesson. I'm not moving.

Not wanting to make him mad, I stand still, looking out into the woods while he walks away.

Is he leaving me? My stomach drops. Shuffling behind me helps calm me. I hear a bag unzip. I'm still frowning when Ajax returns.

"Arms," he instructs, holding out his hand.

Quickly, I shake my head and step back, away from him and his rope.

Ajax sighs. "Louise."

I gulp at the use of my full name.

"So far, you've done very well. I'm very happy. Let's not ruin that," he says, lifting a brow. "Arms," he repeats.

"I'll be good. Please, Ajax, I won't run. Please," I cry.

He sighs again and shakes his head.

Snatching my wrists one after the other, he winds the rope around tightly, securing them together.

"I know you won't run"—he nods—"because your tits are out and so is your freshly fuck cunt."

I flinch at his choice of words.

"And if you run, people will see them. See what I did, what you let me do." Feeding the final loop, he pulls it tight, winding the long remaining rope around his wrist. "What you begged me to do, Lulu."

I swallow more tears. *He's right.* Humiliation rolls

through me. I don't fight as he leads me by the rope, trailing him slowly, my bunched pants not allowing me to rush.

We walk past my stepfather like he's not there. Blinking quickly, I breathe through my mouth to avoid the smell of blood. Only instead of smelling it, I can taste it. It's so thick in the air that there's no escaping.

Together, we head toward my house in silence, my sniffles and cries the only thing punctuating the snapping of the twigs beneath our feet.

Ajax doesn't look at me. Focusing ahead, he keeps a steady stride while I shuffle behind. The excess rope hangs loosely between us. I could pull it and run, but then what? Like he said, everyone would know.

Even as I think it, another part of my brain, the part that begged him to fuck me, whispers in the back of my mind that I don't want to run. Where would I go? I have no one. My mother will never forgive me for this. She loved Andrew more than she ever loved me.

I stayed because I wanted to be a part of a family, but now I really do have no one. I'm alone.

My feet stop, halting our little march back to the house. The rope pulls tight as Ajax continues walking.

"Lulu," he warns, turning.

His eyes roam over me, assessing but one look at my face, and his expression softens. "What's wrong?"

I give him a look.

He's kidding, right?

Ajax rolls his eyes. "Aside from the obvious." His hand waves up and down my body.

"Nothing," I mumble with a shrug.

His chest expands with a huge sigh before he steps closer. Strong fingers pinch my chin. "I thought I made this clear when we met. I do not allow lying in this family."

His tone makes my mouth dry.

"Now, I'll ask again. What's wrong?"

My eyes drop away from his. "I won't have anywhere to go. My mom will hate me when she finds out about Andrew. I'm not ready to be alone." Despite my best efforts, I cry.

Gentle fingers wipe at my tears. "Neither of those things will be a problem for you, Louise."

My brow furrows.

"You, me, and Mary Lou are a family now. There may even be a fourth member soon."

His thumb wipes my cheek, his other hand dropping to my bare stomach.

My eyes widen.

Careful what you wish for.

Ajax tilts his head, watching my mind race. Thankfully, he can't see how my heart pounds, but he might actually hear it at this rate.

If I go with Ajax, I won't be able to come home. I've never been outside of Cromwell Town. But I'll also have a family, a real family.

He's a killer!

He saved me!

What the fuck am I going to do?

Another cold breeze swipes through the trees again, biting painfully at my skin. Shivering, I make a decision, for now at least.

Raising my shoulder, I wipe my nose and cheek on it. With one last sniffle, I start walking home again. Ajax nods, a pleased smile creeping across his mouth as he leads me back, walking a little closer than before.

CHAPTER THIRTEEN

Ajax

The house is dark, just as I left it. Reaching into my pocket, I take out the back door key. I couldn't risk anyone finding my earlier prey.

Lulu stops beside me. Shifting uncomfortably, she pushes to her tiptoes and peers inside the house, probably wondering where her mom is.

I smirk. I was going to tell her that her mother had been punished, but if the fear of being rejected by her mom keeps Lulu compliant, then the death of the woman upstairs can stay my little secret.

"Settle," I order.

Her feet drop flat on the ground. My eyes roam over her again. Although still gorgeous, my girl is turning a concerning blue. It's time to warm her up.

I raise a finger to my lips. "You're going to be

quiet. We're going to creep upstairs, where you will do as you're told. I'd hate to wake your mother." *What she doesn't know . . .*

Lulu's eyes bulge. Her hair flails as she nods quickly.

Unlocking the door, I gesture for her to go in.

Keeping her bound, I lead. If it dawns on her that I know my way around, she doesn't say anything. Instead, she continues to be the obedient woman I need and remains silent as ordered.

Once in her room, I close the door behind us. Lulu's eyes flicker to the wall between her bedroom and her parents.

Stepping close, I keep my voice low. "Do you have a bag?"

Her tied hands point at the small wardrobe. A case sits on the top shelf. I point at the bed, and Lulu plants herself on the edge, hissing as the handmade quilt presses against her tender skin.

I don't release the rope, not even as I pull down the case and a duffel bag from beside it.

Looking around the small room, I'm happy that we should fit most of her things in here.

Trapping the rope between my thumb and palm, I lift my forearm, looping the rope under my elbow as I walk closer to her.

It's now or never.

I need Lulu to pack her things before I go take care of cleaning up our problems. They're going to be found. I want them to be found. Just not before I get rid of any DNA, along with any evidence that Lulu was still here.

Her stepfather was aggressive in front of everyone yesterday, so the local sheriff's office should have no problem believing my girl ran away.

All of the excess rope is rolled around my arm, and Lulu raises her hands, her face hopeful. I chuckle as I untie her.

"In a second, you will pack anything sentimental, along with the majority of your clothing. Start with your favorite items, please," I add as a gesture.

Lulu worries her bottom lip.

"Say it," I encourage.

She hesitates but finally whispers, "I can't go with you, Ajax. My life is here. I have to stay. Everyone will be looking for Andrew. I'll leave you out of it," she rushes. "I won't tell them it was you. I'll say you wore a mask. I'll say it was the Halloween killer." Lulu nods. Oblivious to my furious face, she repeats, "I'll say it was him."

My hand shoots up to circle her neck. "Everyone will know that it was me. You're not staying, Louise. You'll travel with Mary and me until we all head home. Where you will be my wife and the mother of my children, including Mary Lou."

Her now free hands claw at my wrist, panicking as my hand restricts her airflow.

"You will treat Mary as if you birthed her yourself. Am I clear?"

Lulu nods frantically.

I tighten further.

"Yes, sir," she gasps out.

Good, that's good.

Her wriggling body draws my attention. My cock twitches at her blood-streaked flesh, her tits bounce. My want for her builds.

Thankfully, the heat of the house has taken some of the blueness from her skin. But she still needs to warm up.

I'd have clothed her, but her words of denial demand humiliation be what warms her. A shower would be best, but I can't risk any of my DNA sticking around.

"This could have been different," I advise. "Lying will be punished, trying to leave will be punished, and disobedience will be punished." I lay down the rules, loosening my grip.

Dropping to a crouch, I unlace and remove her sneakers. Her leggings and panties go next. Folding them carefully, I place them in the duffel bag.

"Stand," I direct, pleased when she does so without complaint. "Arms up." Again, Lulu doesn't fight.

Her once white tank is now covered in smudges of red and brown. I separate the bra and throw it in with her pants. Balling up her top, I find a part of the cotton that's still white. Holding her waist, I reach between her legs and wipe roughly.

Whimpering, Lulu moves to the balls of her feet,

trying to escape my hand, which earns her a swat to her ass.

The slap rings out loudly. Lulu looks at the bedroom wall and settles quickly. Folding her tank for another clean spot, I wipe her again, spearing her with two fingers and curl them toward myself. I can't risk anything dripping out of her.

I hadn't thought ahead. I knew we'd fuck tonight, but I had wanted us back in my RV, safe from consequences.

Carefully, I place the cum-soaked shirt in the bag, then fold the quilt that Lulu had sat on. Situating the suitcase on her bed, I fold the blanket and place it on the open lid.

Lulu runs her hand over it. "It was my dad's. My grandmother made it for herself when she was pregnant with him. Dad had it when she passed. It's the only thing I have of his."

My heart pulls. "Then I'm glad it's coming with us. Anything else?"

Lulu shakes her head.

"Then pack your clothes."

I step back near the door, my feet shoulder-width apart and my arms crossed.

Her eyes study me for a second before doing as I ordered. Drawer by drawer, Lulu picks out what she wants to take.

"Where are the denim overalls from yesterday?"

"In the wash basket." She points, pausing in her packing.

"Don't stop." Sidestepping, I slowly remove myself from the only exit but keep my eyes on her. If she runs, I'm ready, and she won't like the consequences.

Reaching into the basket, I pull out a handful of items, including the overalls. I hold them out for her to take. The other items are two T-shirts, a pair of blue panties, and one sock.

Having touched them, I throw them into the case too.

CHAPTER FOURTEEN

Lulu

Picking up the picture frame from my bedside, I smile sadly.

I wish I could say goodbye.

Three girls stare back from the photo. My two best friends, Sam and Shelby, and me. The three of us were inseparable in school, and then life happened. I regret not making more time for them.

Swallowing hard, I turn to Ajax, my face heating as our gaze meets. His eyes haven't left me since I started. My skin has long warmed but not through the heating nor embarrassment. I look good. One glance at his crotch tells me that he agrees.

What will happen between us when we leave? *Will he take me again? Will I let him?*

Squeezing my legs closed, I fidget.

Shame. That's what warms me.

Ajax smirks, his eyes fixed to where my body betrays me.

"Write a note." He nods to my dresser, where a notepad lies. "Say how Andrew was cruel and that you can't take it anymore. Write that you're leaving this afternoon. Then date the top of the page like a diary."

My mind shuts down as I follow his order. I don't think; I just write the words he tells me.

Standing behind me, Ajax strokes his hand over the back of my hair. My body thrills at his touch.

Taking the finished note, he folds it before placing it on the nightstand.

Please don't open the stand drawer.

Something on my face must give me away because that's exactly what he does.

I grimace. "It was a joke gift. I've had it for years."

Chuckling, he lifts the small vibrator and makes a show of throwing it into the case to come with us.

"I need to go move Andrew and clean up the mess we made."

I cringe as he stresses the word *we*.

"I need to be quick, and it needs to be perfect, so you'll stay here."

I shake my head before he even finishes.

"What did I say about disobedience, Louise?"

I open and close my mouth.

"What if my mom wakes up?" I ask, desperate to find a reason we should stay together.

"She won't," he argues.

My stomach sinks. If he leaves, I won't have a reason not to go to the sheriff. I can't stay here and pretend this isn't happening.

As if he can read my mind, Ajax comes closer. Taking out my grandmother's quilt, he zips up both the case and the bag. Once he's placed them on the floor, he spreads the quilt over the whole bed.

What is he doing?

My breathing grows heavy when he picks up the rope.

"No, no, no." I shake my head, backing up.

"Lulu," he warns.

I don't want him to tie me up again. "I'll be good. I'll stay here. I promise."

His large hands capture my wrists. "I know you will," he agrees, causing me to cry. "Shh," he reminds me. "One day, this won't be necessary. But today is not that day. I won't be long, and then we'll leave."

My tears fall harder.

The rope is tight like before, binding my hands together. Encouraging me onto the bed, Ajax guides me to lie down. His larger form joins me on the bed, straddling my hips. Leaning over, he loops the rope through my old bedframe. The base creaks with our weights, and the metal whines when he pulls tight.

It's too much. The way the rope bites into my skin, the softness of the quilt beneath me, the brush of his clothes against my naked skin, the knowledge of where we are, and that I need to stay quiet. My body reacts without permission. My hips lift, seeking him as Ajax crawls down my body and off the bed.

"Fuck," he curses. "We don't have time." His face looks pained as he shifts his crotch.

Embarrassed, I close my legs, but the friction it causes only makes things worse.

Ajax takes one last look at me and then turns for the door. "I'm not going to gag you or tie you down more. Don't make me regret that, Louise." He doesn't wait for a response, leaving me to blink after him.

With nothing else to do, I lie here reprimanding myself for tonight's events.

I fucked a killer.

My mind replays everything that happened. The deep aches in my body tells me it wasn't some sick dream.

It really happened. All of it.

Ajax's words about my mother not waking sneak back in. *What did he mean?* Fear churns my tummy.

Andrew was different. He deserved it. *Ajax wouldn't harm her, right?* My heart stops at the thought.

My neck bows as I stretch to glance at the wall behind my bound hands. I should check. Maybe she's passed out drunk, and that's what Ajax meant.

Tugging at the rope, I cringe at the noise it makes. Stilling, I hold my breath, waiting for movement that says I woke her, but nothing comes.

Maybe she left to stay somewhere else for the night? *She doesn't have anywhere to go.*

I pull again and again. Almost frantic, I jostle the

knot back and forth as if it will somehow undo the bind.

Suddenly, a loud clang sounds, and my hands pull backward as the headboard drops, separating from the bed.

I roll onto my stomach and onto my knees.

Holy shit.

Climbing off the bed, I grasp the top end of the mattress and pull, shoving my weight into the side at the same time. Slowly, the base and mattress move enough for me to shimmy between the headboard and the bed.

The metal is worn and cheap. The two screws that attached it to the base have pulled loose. The metal slats are long but don't connect to each other. I can slide the rope off the end of the slat that I'm tied to.

My eyes tear up.

Breathing heavy, I make my way to the next bedroom and pause, standing there until my feet ache.

Reaching out, I grasp the doorknob. Turning, I push it open.

All air leaves me.

The sight before me tears me apart. Horrified, I suck in a lung full of air and scream at the same time that a hand latches onto my face, covering my mouth. The sound comes out muffled.

Thrashing, I fight his grip. The smell of blood surrounds us. Kicking my legs, I fight with everything I have.

He killed her!

He didn't have to; she wasn't like Andrew.

Despite my struggles, Ajax manages to corral us into my bedroom. Seeing my bed, he chuckles, the sound vibrating through his body and into mine.

"Little shit."

An arm worms across my chest and the other scoops under my legs. Lifting, he tosses me onto the bed. My breasts bounce, reminding me that I'm naked.

Fury runs through me. Whatever he thought was happening isn't. Fuck him! And fuck his rules!

Jumping off the bed, I make a run for the door, but he catches me easily, throwing me back onto the bed.

"We don't have time for this," he growls.

Snagging the end of the long rope, Ajax tackles me, laying us out on the mattress. He pins my hands above my head when I try to swing my closed fists at him, but my knee connects with his side, forcing a grunt from him.

Straddling me, he traps me beneath him. Even as his weight pushes me into the bed, I try to knee him in the back.

One minute, my hands are tied in front of me, and the next, I'm on my stomach with my hands being retied. Ajax swings his leg over to kneel on one side of me. Grasping my ankle, he bends my leg at the knee, weaving the rope around one foot at a time until I'm lying face down, my hands and feet bound together near my ass.

It's uncomfortable and awkward. I tell him so.

"Then you should have thought about that before you had your little tantrum."

My mouth drops at his words.

"I told you; disobedience has consequences in this family, Lulu," he reminds me.

Turning my head, I watch as he climbs off the bed.

As if my current state wasn't punishment enough, the asshole slaps my ass. The sounds of his palm hitting my bare skin is loud.

Bending at his hips, he braces himself on his knees. "I'm going to put your mother with your step-father because that's where she belongs. She chose him over you, Lulu. Many times."

I turn my face the other way. I don't want to hear this.

Ajax sighs. "I'm choosing you, Lulu. Now and always. There is nothing and no one that will ever separate us. Think of that while I clean up this mess."

A tear breaks free. Rolling over my nose where is drops to the cover below.

The wheels of my case catch on the doorframe before my only exit clicks closed.

Lying here, I think of how different things would be if I had told someone. Made an official complaint with the sheriff, went to live with the Cromwells like Sam offered, or even if I had run away at eighteen like I always wanted. But instead, I chose to stay, to see if my mom would love me if only she saw what a good daughter I was.

This is my fault. All of it is because of me.

One tear turns to many, and as Ajax moves around my parents' room, I don't try to tame or quieten my sobs. I let them out until eventually I have nothing but exhaustion left.

CHAPTER FIFTEEN

Ajax

My chest heaves with a sigh.

I'm tired and hadn't meant to be out this long. My eyes take in the naked and bound woman sleeping on the bed.

She's worth it.

My mind moves to Mary, but I remind myself that my little girl is okay. The vehicle itself is alarmed so much I'd hear it from here if someone entered.

Not to mention, I was just there dropping off Lulu's things. No one had tripped any of the sensors near the RV. Not what I had planned but the extra trip was necessary with Lulu's current state of mind. The question now, is how do I get my girl there without waking the whole town?

The fact that she's sleeping helps, I smirk.

Her body looks awkward and I know she'll be sore when she wakes. Nothing she doesn't deserve. I just hope that Lulu is a quick learner. I don't enjoy doing this, but I will as many times as I need to.

We have to leave town, soon. I'd go now but when two murders happen in a small town, people tend to be suspicious of those that leave before the bodies are found. After, that's not too bad, especially for visitors.

Who wants to be in a town where a killer is on the loose?

We'll use the frantic energy of the town to leave without suspicion tomorrow.

I sigh again as I climb onto the bed. Something tells me it won't be that easy.

CHAPTER SIXTEEN

Ajax

We make it back to the campsite before my wife-to-be wakes. Wrapped in her grandmother's quilt, she doesn't have the option of flailing about.

Sleepy brown eyes blink up at me. Turning her head, she glances around, making a noise of concern.

"Shhh," I soothe.

We're so close; in a few more minutes, I'll have her in our home away from home.

Resigned or too tired to fight, Lulu lowers her head back to my shoulder and settles the rest of the way to my RV. Grateful, I drop a kiss to her head.

Peering out of the woods, I make sure the coast is clear before stepping out into the open. The RV is parked close to the trees and in the corner of the lot, but we're still exposed for the few steps it takes to get to the door.

Careful of the sensors, I step over the invisible line coming from the plant pot, one of many surrounding the van. Although soundless, it trips the first of three triggers for the RV to go into full shutdown. Metal shutters slamming over the windows are bound to bring attention, along with questions that I can't answer.

I set Lulu on her feet so that I can dig out the key. Sliding it into the lock, I avoid the handle. That being the second trigger.

Wrapping my arm around Lulu's waist, I lift her off the ground. We need to be quick. Opening the door won't set off the system, but it will sound the alarm. We have four seconds to get in and input the code.

I open the door and rush us inside, then close it quickly and quietly. The keypad is right here, the light red. One, nine, zero, enter. The light turns green.

I lock the door, the sound of four locks turning into place suddenly louder than usual. Finally, I use the key, securing the last lock.

I need to see Mary.

Pocketing the key, I turn and hold out my hand. "Let's go check on Piglet."

Lulu eyes the door, then looks back at me.

Please don't fight, I silently plead. I'm exhausted. I need a shower, bed, and a good fuck. Not in that order.

Remembering her bloodstained skin beneath the quilt, I feel my trousers grow tight. It's a shame it has to go, but there can be no evidence of what happened tonight.

Shower first it is.

A slim arm peeks out from between the folds of the blanket. Her hand slips into mine. Pleased, I give it a firm squeeze.

Quietly, I lead Lulu to the left, through the kitchen and living room, down a narrow hall that houses Mary's room. Creaking the door open, I glance in, happy when I find Mary Lou sleeping soundly. I've never been more grateful for the fact that once that girl is out, she's out.

I'd normally sneak in for one more good night kiss to her head on my way to bed, but it's nearing six o'clock. I still need to sort Lulu, and hopefully, we can catch a few hours of sleep before Piglet wakes up.

I'm hoping she'll sleep longer if I don't wake her at our usual eight.

Closing the door, I lead Lulu farther down the small hall, past the bathroom and to the end door.

Our room.

Pushing the door open, I motion for her to enter first.

Again, she doesn't fight.

Lulu stops near the edge of my bed, her lip disappearing between her teeth. I point at the door on the end wall. Her hair, now matted and dirty, flies out wildly as she twists to follow my finger.

"I'll take that." I motion to the blanket.

When she makes no move, I practically have to pry it from her fingertips, making me chuckle.

I fold the blanket, placing it across the bottom of the bed. It can go in the laundry with my clothes and the towels we use in a minute. Encouraging her to the bathroom with a firm hand on her back, I turn on the shower, close the toilet lid, and sit down to unlace my boots, my jacket soon joins them on the floor.

Without encouragement, Lulu steps into the shower. Warm water washes over her, pooling pink at her feet.

The glass door between us steams quickly, hiding her from view, and it shatters my self-control. My plan to clean up while she showers and then to have one myself after goes out the window. The blurry shape of her body and the way she keeps looking over at where I sit is too much to ignore.

Standing, I reach behind my head and pull my shirt off. The rest of my clothes join the pile waiting to be cleaned.

The shower is barely big enough for both of us, but I manage. Together, we wash off her body. Our hands bump, her body shivering at the attention I give it. Mud washes off me, mixing at our feet with the bloody water. The sight has my cock seeping.

I can't believe she's mine.

Cupping her breasts, I kiss the back of her neck. After the night I've had, it won't take long for me to explode. One dip in her tight channel will do it. I'll make it up to her later.

Lulu pours shampoo onto her hair, scrubbing her scalp.

My chest heaves with need. Stepping closer, I press my chest to her back, and her head barely touches my shoulder.

I kiss her neck again. One hand massages her breast while the other drops to steady my cock. Bending my knees, I tilt my hips and push into her to the hilt, buried deep within a second.

Her gasp gets lost in the noise of running water.

I was right. That's all it takes.

As soon as our hips are flush, my pleasure spills into her. Holding her tight, I fill her. Panting, I kiss her shoulder.

Lulu shifts her hips, probably sore from our earlier fucking, but I just hold her tighter. My right hand drops to her lower tummy, keeping her still.

Pulling out, I straighten, dropping another kiss on her shoulder when she whimpers. I'm a big guy, both in length and thickness. It'll be a while, if ever, before she takes me without any pain.

Her hair rinses out quickly, and I pause my touches of her just long enough to scrub my own hair.

I am more than ready for bed, and by the redness of her skin, so is Lulu.

Shutting off the water, I step out first.

I dry her body, patting the water from her arms

and chest. Dropping down, I wipe her legs, happy to see my cum leaving her.

I'll have her pregnant before Christmas.

"Are you on birth control?" I blurt out.

Lulu blushes, glancing down at me. My chest relaxes when she shakes her head.

"Good," I praise, leaning in to kiss her mound. Wide-eyed, she watches me. She's not fighting me, and that's all that matters.

Drying her hair, I squeeze the water from the brown strands, the ends curling as I release them. Once she's dry, I turn the towel to myself.

I'm satisfied and calm to a level I have never reached before. I thought Lulu would struggle to sleep after her earlier nap, but as soon as she climbs beneath the sheets, her eyes close and her breathing settles.

I practically have to drag myself into the bathroom to clean up, but all evidence needs to go. Thirty minutes later, I join Lulu in bed, pulling her close.

CHAPTER SEVENTEEN

Ajax

A sharp beep pulls me from sleep. A second has me diving off the bed . . . someone is near the RV, near my family.

My heart pounds.

Snatching my cell off the nightstand where it's been all night, I pull up the security cameras from around the van.

Police. A lot of them.

Fuck!

They should be busy at the crime scene I left for them. They're not focused on our van yet, too busy with the one next door. Looks like they're going from lot to lot.

There's nothing for them to find in here . . . except Lulu.

I grab a pair of jeans. "Lulu," I whisper. "Louise," I hiss when she doesn't stir.

The hidden cameras show the cops stepping into the RV next to me. After one last look at the phone where I threw it onto the bed, I make a decision.

Lulu needs to go now.

I press my lower leg against the ottoman at the foot of the bed, shoving it aside with my weight, then lean down and roll the rug. Wood flooring stares back at me. You'd never guess that part of it lifts. No one knows what's below except me and, in a moment, Lulu.

Carefully so as not to scratch the floor, I lift the connected wooden slats. A small compartment appears. I leave the second door locked for a few more minutes. Lulu needs to be ready first.

I hate to access the under compartment from here. It's for desperate times only, but that's what this is.

I grab the black rope from the ottoman. It's probably best cops don't find it anyway.

Time for a rough wake-up call.

Grasping Lulu by the ankles, I tear her down the bed. A short squeal escapes her, but I cover her mouth quickly and slap her naked ass, so she stills quickly. Her panicked breaths hit my hand.

"If one more sound leaves your mouth, I will take off this belt and whip your ass until my arm hurts. Do you understand?"

Lulu nods, rolling her lips between her teeth, but

it doesn't hide her whimper. Despite my threat, I let the sound go. Her body is shaking, so she won't be a problem.

My chest heaves as I drag in much-needed air. I might be rushed, but my hands are steady as I weave the rope around her body.

It's smooth to the touch as it wraps around her chest, framing her breasts. I knot it along her back before looping around the front again. Steadying her arms at her lower back, I secure them. Pulling tight, I lead the two pieces down her ass crack and up between her legs at the front.

Because I am the man that I am, I make sure they lay over her clit. Feeding the rope under the row at her lower belly, I let go long enough to turn Lulu onto her side. Bending her knees, I weave the rope over her thighs, working my way down until they are trapped together and pulled up toward her body.

I see on her face the minute that the rope rubs her pussy. Her eyes widen, and her cheeks flush with more than anger and outrage.

My cock responds at the sight of her. She's wrapped up like a gift, one I'm more than ready to open.

We literally have minutes, and my hard-on is demanding that I fill her. I need it more than I need my next breath.

My phone beeps again.

I need her quiet. Blindly, I grab the first thing I can—a pair of socks. Separating them, I roll one.

Lulu shakes her head.

"Open," I order, pinching her cheeks together.

Lulu fights, trying to turn her head away, but I force the cotton in.

The second door hidden in the floor opens with a click, and the smell of death hits me hard in the face. It only makes my arousal grow.

Thank fuck I went for jeans.

Settling Lulu into the storage below isn't easy. The rope is almost too tight to fit my fingers beneath, and the hole in the floor is too small for both of us. Grabbing one of the knots running along her back and behind her thighs, I carry her the small distance sideways and lower her carefully.

The entrance may be small, but the storage isn't. She'd have plenty of room if she weren't bound so tightly.

A knock sounds just as I close and replace the flooring. Scampering, I move the rug and furniture back, then snag a shirt on my way out.

By the time I get to the front door, I have calmed my breathing. With one last breath, I crack the door open.

Three officers greet me.

"Officers, is everything okay?" I frown, a concerned look in place.

"Why would you think otherwise?" one of them rushes. My eyes drop to his name badge, Maxwell. A badge for Greenover Sheriff's Department also sits on his chest.

"Because you're knocking on my door at . . ." I pause to glance at the clock on the kitchen counter. "Eleven thirty." This time, my frown is genuine.

How the fuck did that happen? I feel like I just closed my eyes. Mary Lou's bedtime will not go easy tonight.

"May we come in?" the shorter man asks.

"I'd rather you not."

All three shuffle at my denial.

"My daughter is sleeping."

Maxwell glances at his watch, probably wondering why we're not up and about for the day at almost twelve.

Me too.

"We had a rough night and didn't get much sleep," I explain.

"Sir, there have been two murders. We're looking at everyone traveling through town," the second man says.

My brows rise at his words, and a gasp falls from my lips. "What? I heard the rumors that there was a serial killing a few years ago, but I assumed it was just that, rumors." I glance back into the RV with a concerned look. "Maybe my daughter and I should head out today. I don't want her around anything . . . dangerous."

The two men get a little twitchy, trying to peer inside.

"No one is allowed to leave town right now. Feds orders." Maxwell glares.

"Perhaps I can come in and have a look around. I'll be as quiet as a mouse," the female officer offers.

"Officer Garcia," I say, making a show of looking at her name badge, "Mary would be scared if she were to wake to a stranger in her room, police or not."

"She'll never know I was here." She smiles.

I twist my mouth, but finally, I nod.

"Her room is the first one down the hall." I gesture.

"Step outside, please, while Garcia goes inside." Maxwell huffs.

I do without protest.

"How far was the murder?" I ask while we wait.

"We can't discuss an ongoing investigation."

You already did, dipshit.

The two men seem happy to stand in silence, so I drop any pretense of small talk.

I've never been this close to the police, not while it's me they're hunting. I didn't think I would find it so . . . thrilling.

The image of Lulu bound and gagged, waiting for me to return, amps me up further. *Everything happens for a reason.*

Stopping in Cromwell Town had been a last-minute decision, one of the best I'll ever make.

Officer Garcia exits my home just as quietly as she entered.

"All clear. No one in there other than the girl. Who is sound asleep," she reassures me. "No signs of blood, and nothing out of place." Stepping down, she turns to me again. "Thank you for your time and patience, sir."

Together, the three officers move on to the next lot.

More than ready to get to my girl, I head inside, locking up tight as I do.

"Daddy?" a sleepy voice calls from the kitchen entrance.

Shit.

"Hey, sleepyhead," I coo.

Mary smiles, rubbing her eyes.

"I'm hungry."

"I bet. You slept so late you could probably eat a horse." I tickle her. "Pancakes or Froot Loops?" I ask.

"Froot Loops!" She grins.

I give one last look toward my bedroom. Lulu is secure and not going anywhere. My stomach flutters at the idea of leaving her down there, but it might be just what's needed to take that last bit of fight out of her.

Can she take it?

The kitchen clock ticks loudly. *A quick breakfast it is.*

"How about breakfast, and then we get ready for a day at the park?" I ask Mary, lifting her onto the counter.

CHAPTER EIGHTEEN

Lulu

Darkness swallows me whole when Ajax closes the door.

No!

The sock in my mouth muffles my scream. Air lodges in my chest, choking me.

Motherfucker!

Last night had been horrific, scary, and a nightmare come to life. Ajax had saved me, and I've been stuck in a weird place ever since.

I wanted him, wanted what he did, but I don't want this.

Ropes bind me. I can't move my limbs. My nipples are beaded, and my breasts are heavy. Even with the smell down here, my body calls for him. The thin rope presses against my clit, igniting me.

I strain, trying to hear something, anything, but it's silent. I can feel someone moving around above me, so they must be in the bedroom. After a second, it stops.

I wriggle, kind of. My eyes widen, and a moan slips out. Excitement leaks out of me.

I hate him. Even furious, I want him. My hatred grows, spreading through my chest with every new wave of arousal.

My vision settles, and my eyes start to adjust. A prone form lies in front of me, and shocked, I scream.

It takes a second for my mind to recognize it.

A deer.

Air whooshes out of me.

Fuck!

I half chuckle into the sock. I roll my eyes and then roll my body. Now that I can see, I don't want to have to stare at Bambi's mom until that jackass decides to free me from this hole.

It takes some rocking, but eventually, I roll, giving the carcass my back.

How is the smell stronger?

My gaze settles again. This time, when I scream, I don't stop. My horror rings out over and over.

Tears and snot mix on my chin as sobs rip out of my chest.

Another prone body stares back. His face is so close that I can see the freckles on his nose. My gaze roams him without permission. He's been shot in the leg and chest, and his throat gapes open. The sight makes me gag.

I tear my gaze up, not able to look any longer, but blank eyes stare back.

I gag again. And again.

My sobs don't stop, and my screams continue until my voice stops working.

Every heave, every movement, every cry makes the rope rub, and my body responds more and more.

My hatred for Ajax grows with every breath, but I hate myself more. Lying next to a murdered man, I'm stuck between pleasure and horror.

This is hell, and Ajax put me here.

CHAPTER NINETEEN

Ajax

Today's mission is to wear Mary Lou out. Otherwise, no one will sleep tonight.

"Okay, baby. You get to choose your outfit, but it's jeans and a shirt, please. Do you need help?"

"No, I can do it." Piglet smiles.

"Good girl. When did you get so big?" I ask, leaving her to pick out her clothes.

After one glance back to confirm she's in her room, I slip into my own.

The sight of my future wife lying bound and gagged in the under-floor storage brings back every bit of excitement I felt putting her there, along with the thrill of having cops at my door. It was almost as good as the kill itself.

My cock lengthens, and my chest heaves.

Lulu refuses to look up at me as I lift her out. Her face is pale except for flushed cheeks, and her body shakes in my arms.

Fuck! It was too much.

"You're okay, baby," I say over and over, placing her on the bed. My hands sweep brown locks of hair away from her tear-soaked face before my fingers of one hand brace her neck while the other frees the sock from her mouth.

"I fucking hate you," she hiccups.

Her words stab me in the chest. I've ruined any progress we made.

I'm so fucking sorry, baby.

Climbing on the bed, I tear at the knots. Making my way up her body, I free her limbs. Threading the rope through the row on her stomach, I gently lift her leg to pull it from where it runs between them.

Wrapping the excess rope around my wrist to keep it out of the way, I start to fight with the next knot when I feel it.

The rope is wet. No, it's fucking drenched. My hands freeze at the bottom of her back. As I still, Lulu starts to cry again, her whole body shuddering as her sobs wrench out of her.

Seems we're not completely ruined after all.

My smirk spreads into a wide smile. One that doesn't leave as I climb off the bed. Lulu's legs curl up even tighter, but it's pointless because now we both know her little secret.

Her body shudders when I press a kiss to her

shoulder. Moving my way up the curve of her neck, I press my lips along her flushed skin.

"I hate you," she whispers again.

But this time, her words miss their mark.

"No, you don't, and that's the problem, isn't it?" I ask, reaching between her thighs.

Lulu squeezes them tight, her knees locked together, but it doesn't stop me. My fingers find her wet and ready.

Her words say one thing while her body says another. Lulu doesn't hate me. She hates that she wants me, and I can work with that.

"Ask me to take you, and I'll make you come." I encourage, nudging her shoulder with my nose. "Say the words, Lulu."

My stubborn girl shakes her head.

The first lesson of the day—I get to decide when she comes. Let's see how quickly she learns it.

Goose bumps spread over her pale skin as my sigh whooshes over it. "Let's see how long you can fight it."

I crawl backward off the bed, tugging Lulu with me until her ass hangs over the edge.

After a sharp kiss on her lips, I roll Lulu onto her stomach. Her bare ass entices me, but I shove down the urge to spank her. My girl will undoubtedly give me a reason to turn her skin red soon enough.

Right now, I need to feel her.

Lulu sighs, relaxing her bound upper body into the bed. She knows what I have in mind.

"Good girl," I praise with a smile.

Unable to resist, my hands massage the globes of her ass.

Her legs look awkward, not long enough for her knees to touch the floor but too tall to rest her feet flat on the floor. When she tries to do just that, I force her hips back to the bed with a steady hand on the bottom of her back.

Fuck, she looks good.

Ready and waiting, her wet pink flesh peeks at me through her legs. Groaning, I rip myself away long enough to retrieve my cell.

Snapping a quick picture, I throw the phone down, screen side up, next to Lulu's head on the bed.

Her gasp only fuels my desire more.

Shit, this needs to be quick. Grappling with my belt, I screw my eyes closed as I free my cock, releasing a gasp of my own.

Fuck.

Shoving my jeans down a little, I practically fall onto Lulu. My left hand shoots out, bracing my weight on the mattress near her shoulder while my right clamps onto the crease at the top of her thigh.

I'm neither slow nor gentle as I shove my way inside her body. A gasp of shock whispers through the room, followed by a mewl as my thick cock fills her. Flutters ripple over my shaft.

This is going to end quicker than I thought.

I take a deep breath and then another, but there's

no stopping what's happening to my body. Pleasure courses through every inch of my muscles.

Fuck it, this is supposed to be a lesson anyway.

Leaning forward, I brace my upper weight more on my left hand, shivering when her bound hands graze the bottom of my abs. The contact makes Lulu moan, and any control I have left snaps.

Quick and harsh, I snap my hips back and forth, burying myself inside her over and over. Our groans mingle with the sound of our hips meeting roughly. Her walls clamp down, strangling my cock.

She's about to come, only she's not.

Pulling out, I gasp. My wet cock stands between us, a missile ready to go off, angry and desperate to be back inside her. Who am I to deny?

"Please."

"Please what, baby?" I ask, not slowing.

"Ahh," Lulu cries out.

"Say it, Lulu. Beg me," I pant.

My right hand lands on the bed, my hips swinging back and forth with renewed vigor. Lulu's body rocks as I plow into her, and my hips smack her ass over and over.

"No? Just me, then."

Pushing up off the bed, I take hold of her hips and look down. Watching a few strokes of my cock hammering into her drenched pussy is all it takes to push me over the edge. Pleasure rips through me and into Lulu. Her body is more than happy to take what

I have, and the wave of her own orgasm starts to peak.

I pull out, shooting cum onto her back, groaning at the sight. *What a waste.* But I am a man of my word, and she didn't beg.

Frustrated, Lulu cries out, kicking her legs. Widening my stance, I avoid her feet and stroke out the rest of my orgasm. Once I'm spent, I lean over, pressing a kiss to her hair.

I thought watching my cum leak out of her was erotic, but the sight of it splattering her back and arms hits me just as much. Panting, I take myself in hand again, wiping the wet tip on the curve of her ass.

How have I lived without this? Without her?

I press one more kiss to her hair, and something in my stomach tightens at the sight of her tearstained face.

"Are you in pain?" I check.

Lulu shakes her head, but her tears don't stop, and her hips shift.

"Out loud, Louise. Other than your pulsing pussy, are you in pain?"

"No!" she growls out.

Good. Frustration never killed anyone. But that attitude will get her another punishment.

"Watch your tone," I reprimand.

"Fuck off, I hate you." Her words are broken by hiccups.

I give a heavy sigh and climb off the bed.

"I need to go out. Mary needs to play, and I need to see what's happening in town," I explain, a first for me.

Gently, my fingers press into the muscles of her arms, wanting to ease out any aches she may feel.

"Can you take it a little longer?" I ask, referring to her bound upper body.

Lulu nods. It's small but enough.

"That's my girl," I praise. "Next time I tell you to beg, you beg. And attitude gets you nowhere in this house."

Leaving her to cry out her sexual frustration, I strip completely. Mary will be waiting since I've already taken too long.

Fully dressed and ready for the day, I grab my other rope and make a mental note to pick up some more. Something tells me we're going to need it. I'm closing the storage door when something tucked in the back catches my eye.

Lulu's suitcase.

My face relaxes into a smile. The woman in question stills at the sound of my chuckle.

Our eyes meet as I head back to her, items in hand. Lulu's eyes drop to see what I'm carrying, horror washing over her face when the realization hits.

Second lesson of the day—there's a fine line between pleasure and pain, and I'm the one who decides which one she gets.

CHAPTER TWENTY

Ajax

Leaving Lulu bound to my bed with her legs spread wide was harder than I expected. Not because the vision of my cum leaking out of her is and will always be one of the best sights I've ever seen but because I want her with us.

I swing Piglet's hand back and forth, causing her whole body to shake, her giggle making me grin. My mind whirls with images of Lulu on the other side of my baby girl, the diamond on her finger gleaming as we swing Mary Lou between us.

Soon, I promise myself.

After a few more lessons, Lulu will be exactly where Mary and I need her . . . with us, permanently and of her own free will.

The RV park being on the edge of town is useful

for sneaking off into the night unnoticed, but my eye twitches the farther away we get.

"You ready for the park?" I ask a still giggling Mary as we head toward the town square.

"Uh-huh." She nods. "Daddy," she says quietly after a few minutes.

"Yeah, baby?"

"Can we go to the store first?"

"The one with Mr. Duke?" I ask, thinking she wants another hot dog. For a gas station, they have really good food.

Mary shakes her head.

"Oh, the grocery store?"

She nods.

"Umm, sure. You want another ball?" I push, trying to figure out her sudden need to go shopping. She loves the park.

"No. Yes," she corrects herself quickly.

I chuckle but leave her answer hanging between us. She obviously has something else to say.

Mary glances up at me. "Maybe Miss Lulu will be there again."

My heart hammers in my chest. Shit, how do I explain this in a street crawling with cops, but I don't get a chance to gather my words before she continues.

"That man was mean."

I stop dead in my tracks, pulling her to a halt. Crouching, I turn my baby toward me and frame her face. "Remember what Daddy said the day before yesterday? What I say all the time?"

Mary frowns. "That I can't have a Piglet?"

My booming laughter catches the attention of a couple walking close by, and an officer at the end of the road looks back at us.

This girl owns my heart. I never knew I could love someone until I brought her into this world.

"No," I say, still chuckling. "That Daddy will fix it."

"Oh." She nods, her lips curving into a small smile, but it doesn't last long. Mary glances down, and her shoulders slump. "My heart's broken. Can you fix that?"

A pain stabs my chest, and just as I'm about to panic, I see it. Her lip twitches. *What is she up to?* "Daddy can fix anything. What do you think will do it?"

"A piglet." She smirks.

My laughter is loud and carefree as it mingles with her cheeky giggles. I tickle her sides, and squeals peel out of her.

A few townies stop and stare with wide smiles. From the outside, we look like a loving family. No one would suspect that I have Mary's new mother gagged, tied, and stuffed with a sex toy that will have her sobbing with pained pleasure by the time we return.

My already wide smile somehow grows even bigger at the thought.

"No piglet for you," I deny.

Standing, I bring Mary with me and pull her close.

"How about ice cream instead?"

"Two scoops," she insists, holding up two fingers.

"You're really in a demanding mood today, huh? How about one scoop with sprinkles, but you have to stay quiet and be a good girl while Daddy talks to the police officers over there? Deal?" I compromise, pointing at where a few uniformed officers and what looks to be a fed stand around the hood of a cruiser.

Mary scrunches her nose and shifts her mouth left to right. "Deal." She nods.

Offering my pinky, we shake on it.

Time to find out what the feds know.

Approaching the car, I recognize Officer Maxwell and head for him. Holding Mary securely in my arm, I raise my other hand and place a finger to my lips, reminding her of our deal. My sassy girl makes a big show of zipping her mouth closed and throwing away the key.

I press a kiss to the side of her head with a chuckle.

"Officers"—I nod, acknowledging the others around him—"I was just wondering if there is any news on the case?"

"We can't discuss an ongoing case," Maxwell rushes, eyeing Officer Smith, who had let slip about the murders earlier.

"Seems like someone already did." A woman glares. Everything about her screams fed—black fitted suit, practical but smart shoes, and the lack of respect for the local law enforcement.

Officer Maxwell looks away.

"And you are?" the fed asks with a raised brow.

"No one." Officer Maxwell waves me off. "His RV is parked on the RV park, and Garcia searched it. Just him and the kid."

At the mention of her, Mary gives a bright smile and an enthusiastic wave before clutching at my neck again. She's practically vibrating. I have a few more minutes before the thoughts of ice cream overrides her good manners.

"This is my daughter. I'm Ajax," I say, offering my hand.

The fed eyes my outstretched hand for a second before wrapping her own around it, giving an overly tight squeeze as she shakes.

"Agent Collins," she mumbles, looking back at the map spread on the cruiser's hood.

Collins. The name doesn't sound familiar, but her face sure is. She's been at press conferences and is a member of the team that hunts the I-90 killer, the newbie. Usually stoic and hard, her face is now soft, and the barely visible smile changes her look completely. The woman is practically giddy.

Her long nail taps down onto the map of the town, no doubt where they found the bodies. Markings for the rail track just above her dark finger confirm it.

I tamp down my own smile. She thinks she's going to bag herself the most notorious serial killer the Northwest has ever seen.

The probie has something to prove.

I wrap my other arm around Mary and pull her closer to my chest. *I won't be the one who helps her do it.*

Officer Smith sees the gesture. "It wasn't anywhere near your home." He smiles.

"Officer Smith," Collins snaps.

Smith swallows hard, giving me a sheepish shrug when the agent looks away.

I nod my thanks with a small smile. He has no idea how helpful he's being.

"Do you think he left town by hopping on to a train?" I ask, gesturing to where Collins just circled the track markings.

That gets me her full attention. Standing tall, Collins turns to me. "He?"

"They usually are, right?" I shrug.

"Sir, this is really none of your business." She huffs, folding the town map.

"If we're stuck here, it is," I argue. "Officer Maxwell said that we couldn't leave town. The idea of staying with a madman in town isn't really appealing. But if he's gone . . ."

"You can't stop people from leaving, agent," a new voice snaps.

A man in his late forties or early fifties storms closer, dressed in a uniform similar to the Greenover officers.

Collins rolls her eyes. "I need to get to the station. My team should be here soon."

"Your team?" Maxwell smirks.

"Yes," Collins snaps. "I work as part of a team that hunts serial—"

Coughing loudly, I jut my head at Mary, but that only irritates Collins more.

"Killers," Collins finishes loudly.

"Daddy?" Mary whispers.

"It's okay," I soothe.

Fucking bitch.

"Daddy will fix it," I promise.

The new man comes closer. "I'm sorry about that, sir." He sighs, looking at a restless Mary. "Agent Collins is . . . eager. I'm Sheriff McCallister."

I shake his hand. "Not your fault, but I think it's best that I get this one to the park as promised." Setting Mary down, I take her hand and look at the sheriff's badge as I straighten. Cromwell Sheriff shines in the winter sun.

"Sir," the sheriff calls.

Pausing, I turn, and he rakes his hand through his hair.

"Collins's boss is due soon. I'll talk to him. Give me a few hours. We'll have you out of town by nightfall."

I give one last nod and lead Mary away.

I fucking hope so.

CHAPTER TWENTY-ONE

Lulu

"Daddy, Daddy, Daddy, Daddy, Daddy, Daddy," a small child chants.

Mary. They're back.

My heart jumps. More tears spill out when I close my eyes.

Thank you, God.

Hearing their loud voices does nothing to distract from the waves of pleasure that wreck my body. Another tide hits me at the same time I feel the front door slam closed.

"Mary Louise, you stop right there," Ajax booms.

"Awww," Mary says.

All breath leaves my body. *Please don't come in here!* Panicked, I wriggle, tugging at my binds.

"You know better than to run into my bedroom, young lady."

Now they're both right outside. My eyes widen as I fight off another wave, but just like the others, it's useless. My body doesn't belong to me anymore. It belongs to him.

"I think we should have gotten the ice cream before the park." Ajax sighs. "Go grab a game and then pick a film. "Daddy has a surprise for you." I can hear the grin in his voice.

"Yay!"

I want to scream in celebration too when the bedroom door starts to open.

Please release me. I'll be good, I silently beg.

Ajax slips into the room through the small gap before shutting the door tightly.

"Hi, baby," he greets, joining me on the bed.

Unable to speak, I blink at him over my shoulder. Strong fingers wipe at my wet cheek. My body quivers, and my legs shake as another orgasm hits.

His chuckle drowns out my moan.

Ajax tucks my hair behind my left ear. He's gentle and sweet. His hand sweeps down the center of my back, tracing the arch. My hips lift when he reaches the top of my ass.

I continue to blink up at him, watching as he leans back, turning his head to look down at where his hands now grip my ass cheek.

I make an alarmed sound that's muffled by the

gag and has zero effect on Ajax. He pulls my ass cheek, spreading me wide.

"Looks like you made a mess." He tuts.

Craning my neck to meet his gaze, I drop my eyes to his wide smirk.

"Painful?" he asks when I come again.

I blink teary-eyed, then drop my head heavily to the pillow. Humiliation rolls through me.

The vibrator starts to leave me, but my hope is short-lived. The length shoves back in, the vibration jumping up a level.

I cry out in pain as yet another orgasm is forced from me.

"Please," I beg, the word distorting around the material in my mouth.

Ajax pulls the toy out and shoves it back in again and again. I glance back, more than willing to plead, but his eyes are glued to where he penetrates me.

"One more," he orders.

My breathing picks up, and my body responds to him without permission. Something tells me it will always be this way between us.

It's that thought that shoves me over the edge of the precipice. I cry out, a sound that only gets louder when he pulls the toy from me.

My inner walls ripple, and my womb twists, desperate to be filled.

Images of babies and my swollen belly force a sob from me. I turn my face away from him, hiding my horror, pain, and humiliation—but most of all, it smothers my secret.

I want it. I want him. I want a family.

I stay silent, the odd sniffle leaving me as I'm set free.

Ajax straddles my body, taking his time to rub my limbs and soothe the pain, but the deep muscle ache stays.

My legs feel like they're made of jelly as Ajax helps me off the bed. His lips tease mine after he removes the gag.

"Good girl. You'll make a great wife, Lulu."

I feel a thrill at his words. Does he really think that?

I watch as he retrieves a dress from the wardrobe. Frozen, I wait for an order. My mind feels empty, blank. An odd calm consumes me.

"Arms up."

I do as I'm told. Ajax rewards me with a solid kiss.

"You're going to give me babies, Lulu. Lots of them."

His wide grin greets me as my head pops through the dress, his hands gentle as he feeds my arms through the sleeves.

The yellow-flowered material of an old sundress that I haven't worn for years isn't soft like I remember. Instead, it scratches at my overly sensitive skin. My beaded nipples hurt at the contact, causing my breath to hitch.

Ajax chuckles and flicks one, making me hiss.

"Stay," he orders, and I'm more than happy to comply.

Chewing my bottom lip, I try to peer into the bathroom, but I can't see what he's doing. The water runs for a second and then shuts back off.

Ajax returns with a washcloth in his hand.

My cheeks heat, and I shake my head back and forth when his intention becomes obvious.

A growl leaves his chest when my foot lifts off the floor, and I lower it immediately.

Shit.

Ajax glares, gathering the skirt of my dress and holding it at my waist. He reaches between my legs and mops up the mess I made.

How humiliating.

My face flames. I rip my watery eyes away from his serious features and pick a spot on the ceiling to focus on.

Maybe it won't be so bad if I don't look. But the minute Ajax shifts my dress back into place, I know that isn't the case.

I push out a slow and steady breath. Ajax swallows it, and his lips consume mine. His tongue teases, his fingers mean as they grip the nape of my neck.

I give as good as I get, but it's worthless because Ajax was never going to let me win. He devours me.

And I enjoy every second of it.

By the time we separate, I'm wet again. Breathless and needy.

My body is so close. I just need a little push.

I look up at him from beneath my lashes, my arousal openly displayed on my face.

"Not yet. When we put our baby girl to bed, you're going to crawl into my lap and ride me until I fill you up," he demands breathlessly.

I nod, more than ready.

"Yes, please."

Confident fingers smooth my dress over my waist. His hands drop, cupping my ass.

Our panted breaths mingle as our foreheads press together.

"There is a very fine line between pleasure and pain, Louise. You're mine, have been since I saw you at the store. I decide what you feel, and when and where you feel it."

"Yes, sir." I nod, eager to agree.

Ajax gives me one more kiss, and then another. He makes a pained noise as he separates us. Glancing down, a new wave of blush covers my neck and chest, my whole body heating at the sight of his straining erection.

His hand reaches out for me. "You will behave. You will not upset Mary, and you will act like you have always been here . . . Like you want to be here, or the pleasure you want so badly will never come," he threatens, glancing down at where my thighs try to ease my need.

But his threat isn't necessary. I want to please him. I want to stay.

"Yes, sir," I readily agree as he leads me out.

"Uhhh, you took so long, Daddy," Mary complains from the living area.

I hold Ajax's hand tighter as we approach the end of the hallway.

Why am I so nervous?

My tongue brushes over my bottom lip.

"Daddy . . ." Mary turns, freezing the minute she sees us, sees me.

Her little round eyes lock on me, and the room fills with silence. And then a scream.

"You did it! You fixed it, Daddy!"

Mary runs at us. I release Ajax's hand just in time to crouch and catch her. She flies into my arms. Her squeal of joy deafens me, but the look on her face is more than worth the ringing in my left ear.

I glance up at her father. My heart lurches at the way he's looking at us, and I know without a doubt that I am going to hell.

Holding Mary tighter, I screw my eyes shut and embrace my thoughts.

I love her, and little by little, no matter how much I know that I shouldn't, I feel myself falling for the man standing watch over us.

"Piglet," Ajax whispers, "Lulu is going to travel with us until we head home."

Mary tears herself away from our hug, her face shrouded in panic. "Then I don't want to go home. I want to stay here."

Her dad drops to a crouch beside us. "I'm sorry,

baby. I should have been clearer. Lulu will be coming home with us."

Now, it's my turn to look panicked. My soul might crave this ready-made family, but I watched this man murder someone. I saw what he did to my mother.

My breath hitches, fear and anger flooding me. As if he can sense it, Ajax rubs my back, then pats my ass.

"She's coming home with us," he says again, his hard gaze meeting mine. A challenge. One I'm not equipped to deal with.

I stutter a breath.

"What game have you picked, baby?"

"Hungry Hippos." Mary grins, rushing away to fetch it.

"I'll play one round, and then I'll cook dinner. You haven't eaten today." Ajax frowns. "A mistake I won't make again. I'm sorry," he apologizes, kissing my lips.

Aware of Mary close by, I try to pull away.

"No," he snaps, gripping the front of my neck. His eyes flick to Mary before his hand slides to the nape of my neck. "You don't pull away," he orders against my lips.

Our kiss is softer than before but not gentle.

"Just for that, you don't come tonight."

I make a sound of protest in the back of my throat. His thumb brushes over the center of my throat. His pupils dilate more when he feels the vibration.

Even with his words, my pussy clenches for the millionth time today, more than willing to have him fill me.

"I'm yellow," Piglet declares, interrupting us.

"What color do you want, baby?"

"Red," I breathe. "Red," I repeat, tucking my hair behind my ears, then turn toward an overly excited Mary.

Joining her on the floor, I touch my heated cheeks. *How far away is bedtime?*

Guilt immediately swarms me. I might be hungry for more than food, but as Ajax joins us, I have never felt a part of a family more than I do right now.

How sad is that?

My stomach flutters, and my heart sinks as I remember my mom. Swallowing hard, I look at Ajax.

His blank stare bores into me, and somehow, I know he senses where my mind has gone. Guilt hits me again, making me frown. I've done nothing wrong, have I?

"Let's play." He smiles at us, but his voice is authoritative, his words an order. And just like earlier, I don't think, I just follow.

Ajax stays and plays three extra games after the first is over. The man really hates to tell Mary no, but after the fourth time, he annihilates us and loudly celebrates, Mary practically shoves him toward the kitchen island.

"Don't let her win," he tells me, picking up a kitchen knife.

"Yay!" Mary cheers, pumping her arms.

Too late.

"Don't be a bad winner, Mary Lou." Her dad reprimands, waving the knife in our direction.

Seems she's very competitive. *Like father, like daughter.*

"Hey," he calls.

Shit, I didn't mean to say that out loud.

I grin sheepishly, and he squints in reply. Mary giggles loudly.

"Let's play again. I like playing without Daddy because I win."

"Not this time, Piglet." I shift to my knees. "I'm gonna kick your butt," I taunt.

Mary's jaw drops, but she recovers quickly, her grin wide as she shifts to mimic my pose.

"Three, two, one . . . go!"

CHAPTER TWENTY-TWO

Ajax

Pride flows through me. Lulu had won every game except the last. Mary's grin rivals my own. Lulu was right—like father, like daughter.

"Good job, baby. You showed her," I call over, winking at Mary.

"Hey!" Lulu protests.

"You did good too, wifey. We'll make a Whitler out of you yet."

Lulu blushes, and Mary's head snaps around, her wide eyes finding me at my words. I expected her to be giddy, her excitement palpable, but instead, her little chin wobbles, and her eyes fill with tears.

"Piglet," I start, my words a whisper, but before I can get any further, Mary turns and launches herself at Lulu for the second time this evening, jumping into open arms ready to catch her.

I hate that I missed it. How could I not see how much Mary Lou needed a mother? Placing the spaghetti down, I walk over and join my girls.

Wrapping them in my arms, I pull them both close.

Mary clings to Lulu. Low tones of her whisper reach out, but the words are lost in Lulu's neck, a secret between my two girls. Lulu's finds me, her gaze beyond sad, and I know it's one I'll let them keep.

"Yeah, Piglet. You're my baby."

Mary whispers something else, the almost silent words making Lulu sniffle.

"I love you too, Piglet," Lulu cries.

I hate seeing them upset. I press a solid kiss to the back of Mary's head, then turn my lips to Lulu's.

"And I love both of you."

Lulu frowns. "You don't have to lie."

Glancing down at our emotional girl, I shake my head. "I didn't lie." I hold her gaze, letting Lulu see the truth.

I do love her. Lulu is a part of this family now. Our missing piece. I'm just pissed that I didn't see it, but even if I had, I wouldn't have thought we'd find it in someone at least fifteen years my junior.

"You okay, baby?" I ask Mary, soothing her back.

She nods her little head, pulling away from Lulu just enough to wipe at her wet face.

"This is better than a piglet," she whispers against her hands.

My heart soars, and by the look on my wife-to-be's face, so does hers.

Lulu kisses her cheek. "I've been called a pig before, but I've never been told I'm better than one." She grins.

She means it as a joke, I know that, but rage attacks me. I wish I could kill her parents all over again.

"You're fucking better than them," I growl against her lips.

Mary gasps. "That's a bad word!"

"It is a bad word," Lulu agrees. "Bad Daddy."

My cock twitches at her words. God, I can't wait for her to give me more children.

"Food and then a film, you two troublemakers." I roll my eyes, reaching to take Mary.

Lulu shakes her head, holding our little girl closer, wanting to carry her.

"What film are we watching?" I ask like I don't already know.

"*Babe*!" Mary cheers, all sadness forgotten.

CHAPTER TWENTY-THREE

Ajax

I look over at the dirty dishes and groan. I don't want to move. I'm content—mind, body, and soul.

Piglet sits cuddled between Lulu and me with a bowl of popcorn in her lap. Sweet and salty, who does that?

Lulu, apparently.

I dip a hand into my own bowl. Tossing a piece and catch it in my mouth.

Mary giggles before trying to copy me. A handful of popcorn rains down on her.

"See what happens when you mix sweet and salty?" I tut. "Here, baby, try this one," I encourage, handing my daughter a few of my own.

She throws them high, and the pieces scatter, but

by some miracle, my sweet girl catches one. Squealing, she sticks her tongue out to show us.

"Yay!" I cheer, my arms shooting up in the air.

Mary laughs, flashing me her chewed popcorn. I cup the back of her head and tilt it forward, even the cringe at the thought of her choking doesn't take my smile away . . . but the knock on our door does.

I shoot up out of my seat, snagging the fork off the top plate. It's sharper than the blunt knives we ate with, so I'll make do.

"You girls, go get ready for bed, please," I say, pointing at the hallway that holds the bedrooms.

"Awwww," Piglet whines.

Lulu swallows when a second knock sounds.

"Pajamas and clean teeth," I tell her with a raised brow.

"But then I can't have more popcorn."

"Mary Lou . . ." I force myself to take a deep breath, bending closer to her height. "Go."

"How about we get you in your pajamas, and I'll brush your hair instead so we can have more popcorn?" Lulu offers as a compromise.

Mary contemplates for a second, then looks at me.

My fingers twirl the fork behind my back. "Fine," I fold.

"Can I sleep in Daddy's room?" Mary asks as they walk to her bedroom.

Lulu glances back at me. I shake my head and call out, "No. Lulu is."

"Awww," Piglet moans, and her little shoulders drop.

A third knock sounds, pissing me off. I glare at my phone on the kitchen counter. I missed the notifications that someone was close. They shouldn't have gotten to the door without me knowing.

I'm motherfucking pissed, yet I have no one to blame but myself.

After one more glance in the direction of my girls, I go to the front door. Sheriff McCallister stands on the other side.

"Sorry to interrupt your night." He smiles.

"No problem, it's bath and bedtime. Everything okay?" I ask, keeping my hand on the door handle. The thought of the three plates on the living room table makes me sweat.

"Yeah, great actually. Well, not great since two people are dead." He grimaces, threading a hand through his gray hair. "I meant I have great news for you. The FBI has agreed to open the roads leading in and out of Cromwell."

The fork clatters loudly behind me.

"Great, thank you for popping by." I start to close the door.

The sheriff looks at the fallen cutlery.

"I was just cleaning up."

He smiles. "A few officers are letting everyone know they're free to leave. The feds are doing car searches," he says, rolling his eyes. "And I'd advise waiting until morning. Everyone's going to be rushing to get on the road tonight." He glances at his watch, and I copy the move.

7:23

Shit, how did that happen? I guess time really does fly when you're having fun.

I glance toward the bedrooms again. McCallister tries to peer around my large body to follow my eye line, but he can't.

"I thought your daughter was in the bath?"

I nod. "She is old enough to want to be independent but young enough that I worry," I explain.

"Your wife isn't with her?"

"I'm not married." I smile, motioning to my ring finger.

Not yet, anyway.

"Say no more." He waves me off. "I have a sister. She's a single parent and the same with her kids."

"Thanks for coming out. It was real nice of you. I think we'll head out tonight. I don't really fancy staying in town, given what's happened. You understand."

"Of course." He nods. "I hope this doesn't put you off returning to Cromwell Town."

"Hmm," I hum with a noncommittal shrug.

"Well, I can't really blame you. Thinking of leaving myself after the past few years." He sighs tiredly. His eyes bulge at his own words.

"I didn't hear anything." I wave away, mimicking his own actions.

He chuckles, shaking a pointed finger at me.

"You make sure to come through the exit that leads straight to the I-90 on the west side of town, a few miles past Duke's station. I'll make sure the boys don't search you. Get you and that little girl of yours on your way."

"I appreciate that. Thank you, Sheriff," I say, trying not to show my delight. I wave, then close the door and lock it.

The girls must have heard the door because they join me in the living room.

"Can we play another game before bed?" Mary asks.

"Not tonight, Piglet. But you do get to stay up late and then sleep in Daddy's bed tonight. Go pick another film," I encourage.

I watch Mary sit in front of our DVD collection. When she's fully focused, I turn to Lulu. "We're heading out. No, not a word," I rush when she opens her mouth. I'm not arguing because I'm not asking. Lulu is coming with us. "You will settle on the sofa and watch Mary while I pack up everything outside."

Lulu nods. She twists her lips but remains silent.

My large hands frame her face. "You're ours now." I kiss her, my lips staying on hers until she responds. "Mary doesn't like to sleep while I drive, so you might have to stay in our room with her tonight."

The little girl in question pushes her way between us. "I picked one."

"Well, we watched *Babe*, so which one have you chosen?"

"*The Little Mermaid*." She grins. I mouth the words to Lulu, and something shifts in my chest when she laughs.

"I've never seen it," she tells Mary, and my baby girl gasps in horror.

"Oh, you're going to regret saying that."

I help settle them on the sofa, collecting and spreading a blanket over them and steal the popcorn bowls away as I leave.

"I wanted more."

"Not tonight, Piglet. You're going to be up late. Snuggle with Lulu and watch the film."

She doesn't argue anymore and instead leans into Lulu's side.

"Stay inside," I order Lulu. "That door doesn't open." I point.

She blinks up at me.

I lean down, my hands on the back of the sofa, my arms bracketing her in, and whisper against her lips, "Say you understand."

"I understand," she repeats. I feel her words more than I hear them.

Fuck, I need to make her fully mine. One day, I'll be able to leave without worrying that she'll run off. *I can't fucking wait.*

CHAPTER TWENTY-FOUR

Ajax

I have us packed up and ready to go in record time.
The cold air helps cool me as I disconnect us from the
site facilities. We'll need to fill our water tanks for the
road trip ahead.

Having planned to be here for another week or so,
I'm not prepared for a long-distance drive.

Who knows where we're headed? Who cares, as
long as it's far from Cromwell? Lulu will settle quicker
if she's away from people she knows.

She will, I reassure myself.

They're both exactly where I left them when I re-
enter the RV.

Perfect.

Walking over, I bend and kiss Lulu. "You did
good," I praise.

Her smile is small, but she can't hide her body's reaction to my words. Her breath hitches, and her nipples bead. Punishment and reward are exactly what Lulu needs, and she craves them. And so do I.

"You ladies staying here while I drive?"

Mary nods, her eyes drooping. I smile, watching her for a second.

"When she drops off, feel free to find something else," I say, handing Lulu the remotes. "We need to fill up on gas, water, and a few food items, and then we're out of here."

"Can I call my friends?" Lulu whispers, ducking her head.

I tuck a finger under her chin to connect our gaze. "No."

She blinks quickly, sucking her bottom lip into her mouth. "Will I ever come back?"

"No."

A tear falls free, and I fight against the instinct to wipe it away. Instead, I watch as it rolls down her reddened cheek, dripping off her chin.

"You don't have anything to come back to. Your family's right here." I nod to Mary, then tilt Lulu's head back, making it easier to connect my lips to hers. "I'm going to give you a good life. How we get there is your choice, Lulu."

She blinks more at my words. "And if I said I don't want this?"

"I'd be very offended," I frown, my voice deepening. "Let her sleep," I order and walk away.

141

Time to get my family out of here.

The queue to get into Duke's is massive. Sheriff McCallister was right; everyone is leaving tonight. I roll my eyes and pull forward, finally being able to enter the parking lot. The old man Duke approaches quickly, and I lower my window.

"You headed out of town?"

"Yes, sir," I answer.

"Your little one asleep for the night?"

"Yeah." I nod. I'm not worried about him seeing Lulu. You can't see in the back with the curtains closed.

"Wait for the car at the front pump to move and then pull up to pump two. I'll fill you up and sort payment for you, save you getting out."

"Thank you," I say, and I mean it. "But I need to go inside and get some food for the road and fill up on water." I nod to the water station.

"We're all out of water." He winces. "But there's a truck stop about an hour that way on the I-90 that has a water station. It's nothing fancy, but they have a bigger facility than us," he suggests.

Shit, I sigh with a frown. My eyes flick to my rearview mirror, but the only thing I see is the black curtain.

"Okay, I'll fill up on gas and grab food." I rub the back of my neck. This is not what I had planned for tonight, but we need to get out of here one way or another.

"I'll sort the gas. You go see Judy about the food." He smiles.

The car at the pump moves, so Duke waves me on before moving to speak to the car behind us.

I climb out of my seat and pop into the back. "I'm going in to pay and get food. The RV will be locked." Walking over, I reach down and hook my thumbs in my belt. "Do you need to go into the bedroom?"

Lulu starts shaking her head before I've even finished my veiled threat.

"I'll be good," she promises, her eyes wide.

I check Mary is sleeping with a glance before leaning down to grip Lulu's chin. "You better. Otherwise, the beating I gave your ass earlier will feel like foreplay."

She flushes at my words, but I'm not done.

"Although by how wet and ready your virgin pussy had been, it was foreplay." I'm being an asshole, but I want her ashamed and scared. Whatever it takes to make her stay. I get exactly what I want.

Shame floods her face, and the sight thrills me. My right hand drops from my belt, adjusting my erection.

When we get to the truck stop, I reassure myself.

I release her chin and head to the door, keys in hand, ready to lock my girls in.

"There you are," Duke calls, joining me at the pump.

I press the lock on my key, locking the driver and passenger door. The old man smiles when he hears it.

"She'll be just fine. I'll be out here, and no one is getting past me."

I nod, appreciating his words, but I won't settle until we're officially out of this town.

My heart is in my throat by the time I'm back in the RV and heading to the roadblock. I can hear Lulu moving around in the back, putting away the few groceries I got.

Fuck, my brow breaks out in sweat the closer the queue gets. It's about a mile long and not moving very quickly. There's no avoiding the blocks set up. Judy was chatting with another customer. Apparently, this queue is the shortest, but the sheriff is why we're here. He better come through.

He does.

My hands are shaking and my breathing short by the time McCallister steps out into the road on the opposite side. His torch flashes as his other hand waves.

I take a deep breath and pray to whoever is listening before pulling out of traffic and heading straight for him.

McCallister motions for me to lower my window, and I do with a smile plastered on my face.

"This one's clean. Let them through, Garcia," he orders into his radio. "Thanks for visiting Cromwell."

I nod my thanks and drive on, giving a small wave out the window as I pass Garcia. My heart hammers painfully and doesn't stop until we're about forty minutes out of Cromwell. We joined the I-90 about thirty minutes ago.

My brain tells me to continue. We can fill up and restock in another town, but another part of me is hard and excited. The thrill of the night is too much to ignore. That part of me wins. A road sign tells me we're close to Cataldo; we can be out of Idaho by midday tomorrow.

It's stupid and irrational, but my hands have a mind of their own as I pull off the interstate. Big trucks litter the parking lot, some closed down and locked up for a good night's sleep while others stand around chatting. It's mostly men, but a few women who are clearly working girls mingle with them.

Heading toward the back, away from sound and witnesses, I park next to a truck with Cromwell Logging written on the hood.

What are the fucking chances? I roll my eyes. This had better not be a sign. Turning off the engine, I take the time to cover the windows and lock my door. Climbing through into the back, I see my girls still cuddled up. Lulu has been so patient with Mary tonight. I couldn't have asked for better.

"I'll take her to bed." I gesture to Mary. "She'll sleep in with us, so we'll fuck out here tonight." Lulu stands at my words. "You did very good at Duke's. Enough that I'll reward you. You won't be denied tonight," I tell her, referring to my earlier threat of not letting her come.

Her chest heaves, telling me she understands my

words. Without saying anything else, I head to our bedroom and change the bedding before I duck back down the hall to retrieve Mary, who remains flat out. She won't wake if I put her in her own bed, but a promise is a promise.

Quickly and quietly, I settle Mary in the middle of my bed, tucking her in tight. Closing the bedroom door, I head to the living area. *I'm so ready for this.*

Instead of being on the sofa, Lulu stands at the sink, flicking the tap off.

Hearing me approach, she turns to me. "Thought I'd do the dishes and clean up."

Walking up behind her, I smirk. "You wouldn't be trying to avoid me, would you?" I ask, my hands gliding up her sides to grope her covered breasts. Her chest lifts and falls quickly, her mouth dropping open when I rub my hips against her ass, letting her feel what she does to me.

Her body shivers, and her nipples pebble, showing me what I do to her. Without feeling it, I know she's wet and ready. I consider lifting her dress right here, but this time, I want to see her face when she feels the sting of taking my fat cock.

A scream outside makes my head snap up out of Lulu's neck.

The fuck was that?

Slipping my hand into the hot water, I retrieve the kitchen knife I used earlier and order, "Stay inside."

The door opens with the view of the logging truck. No other vehicle is nearby. Closing the door, I lock it, not wanting anyone to get in while I'm out. I circle the RV, and from the front, I see the small fire burning where people have gathered, but they seem oblivious to the scream I heard.

Probably not uncommon around here, I think, watching a prostitute leading a trucker into a small brick building, probably the toilets. Seeing enough, I continue around my home. Trees line the edge of the parking lot only a few slots away.

I peer through the trees but see nothing. The back is the same. Giant trees tower over me, giving my family the privacy we need.

I'm about to head back in when I hear another scream. I spin, facing the forest. Leaves rustle. Someone is moving fast. No, they're running. The sounds are moving away, which is all that matters, but it's still too close.

A third scream rings out followed by a moan. *Really? Fucking johns.* Needing confirmation, I wait with my eyes glued to the dark trees.

A tall figure walks parallel to me. It might be dark, but I know what a man carrying a limp body over his shoulder looks like. A giggle rings out.

I turn away, leaving the couple to their games. It's not bothering my family, which means it's not my business.

Besides, I have better things to do than watch some trucker fuck a whore, like sinking into my own woman.

My cock hasn't gone down, my excitement only

growing at the prospect of killing again so soon. I glance at the storage compartment as I head to the main door, which I unlock and open with a smile.

Lulu stands drying the dishes, her lip caught between her teeth.

I flick the last lock and forget about everything outside of these walls. Reaching down, I unbuckle my belt, and my cock's out before I sit on the sofa.

"Come here," I order, panting.

My hand wraps around my aching member. Lulu falters, her motions slow as she folds the towel. "What about filling the water?"

"I'll do it in the morning. I revoked your punishment earlier, Louise, something that I do not do lightly. Here, now."

She reacts instantly, stopping between my spread legs, her eyes zeroing in on my face, refusing to glance down.

"Straddle me and lift your dress. I want to see where my dick pierces you."

Lulu does as she's told. Her upper body is straight as if she's afraid to touch me, but I can see her excitement on her thigh. She's more than ready.

Keeping hold of my arousal, I reach out with my other hand, bringing her closer until I have her exactly where I want, with her wetness hovering over me.

"You may come, but you hesitated," I tut. "And for that, I'm going to fuck you harder than I've ever fucked anyone."

The warning does nothing to prepare her for the force with which I enter her. My eyes stay fixed on her face, wanting to see her pain and arousal, and my woman does not disappoint. Her mouth falls open in a silent scream. Her brows furrow, and her body tenses.

I take her ruthlessly, my gaze dropping to where we're connected. My hands grip her roughly, forcing her to bounce on my lap. Lulu cries out in pleasure, and I know again without a doubt that this woman was made for me.

CHAPTER TWENTY-FIVE

Lulu

My head turns, reading the Riverside State Park sign as we pass it. Washington is beautiful, what we've seen of it anyway. After pulling off the I-90, Ajax headed straight here as if he's been before.

I glance over at the man next to me. The past few days with Ajax have been . . . different. Andrew was always quick to temper, but Ajax warns me before he doles out a punishment. Following orders has been easier than I thought and not unpleasant.

My pussy chooses that time to pulse, reminding me of what else he does often. I shift in my seat, suddenly very aware of the large hand resting on my thigh. Will my body ever not respond to him?

My chest tightens like it does every time I start to remember what he did and how we got here.

"How long are we staying?" I ask, anything to break the suddenly stifling silence.

"A day or so, the same as the other places. Why?"

"No reason." I shrug.

Ajax frowns, his eyes leaving the road to glance at me.

"This is just new is all."

"You'll get used to it." He smiles, squeezing my leg. "Besides, we'll head home in a few weeks."

I don't point out that I no longer have a home. I made that mistake yesterday.

My mouth dries.

Returning his smile, I blink out of the front window, watching the beautiful scenery coming into view.

"You'll like it in Wisconsin. We have a lot of land for the hunting business, but don't worry; the house is secluded and nowhere near the guest accommodation. It'll just be you, me, and Mary. For now, at least." He grins, raising his hand to rest on my belly.

My stomach twists—with excitement or horror, I'm not sure. We've taken no preventive measures, and we're having a lot of sex. If Mary is napping or gone to bed and Ajax isn't driving, he's inside me. Even being on the road doesn't always stop him. I blush at the memory of him pulling to the side of the road on the edge of a small town. The curtain to the front seats was barely closed before he had me on all fours.

The arousal I felt just a few seconds ago ramps up. Ajax isn't the only one with a problem.

"Lulu?" Mary calls from the living room.

"Yeah, baby?"

"Can we wear matching overalls today?"

"Absolutely." I smile.

Ajax's hand squeezes me again.

"They're still ripped."

"I'll fix them." I promise her. "At least I know what I'm doing today," I tell her dad.

Ajax grins as he reverses the RV, parking in the back away from everyone else and close to the tree line, like always.

I watch a family across the way setting up camp and wonder if I should ask for a phone. What would happen to Mary if her dad got arrested? The thought breaks my heart.

"Don't even think about it," he whispers in my ear. "I'd kill them all, and we'd be gone before the police even got here."

I swallow hard and turn to him, our eyes meeting. He means it. He'd kill everyone here to keep me. My chin quivers, and a tear breaks free, not because he'll never let me go but because I want to be here.

The past few days with this family have been the happiest I've ever been. Every day I stay with Ajax, I hate my mother a little more. She did this. She made me need him, want him.

So I don't fight when his lips touch mine. Instead, I lean in.

After all, no one has to know how much I want this, right?

CHAPTER TWENTY-SIX

Lulu

"Alright, Piglet, time to do some schoolwork. Daddy's orders," I call out, grabbing her subject books out of the school supply box.

"Awww." Her groan carries out into the living room, making me laugh.

"Has she ever been enrolled in a public school?" I ask Ajax.

"No." He shakes his head, not glancing up from the laptop he's typing on. "I need to be able to travel whenever I need a . . . release." He hesitates, his eyes meeting mine.

I gulp at what I see, pleasure and anticipation.

"I refuse to leave her at home. I can't protect her if I'm not there." He frowns, turning back to his work.

"What . . . what about her mom?" I whisper, chewing my lip.

His fingers freeze on the keyboard, and my heart stops. Ajax slowly lifts his eyes, blazing a trail up my body.

"Gone," he answers shortly.

Why did I open my big mouth? Stupid, stupid, stupid.

I stand frozen. Ajax continues to stare, his anger obvious. Andrew would have beaten me by now. I wait for Ajax to stand and advance, but he doesn't. Instead, he blinks and turns back to his emails.

My hands are shaking as I thumb through the books.

"English, science, and math today, please."

His politeness after seeing such anger on his face throws me off, and I don't know what to do. Chewing my lip, I pull out the books he wants.

I flinch when his large hand covers mine, his body looming as he stands beside me.

"You're mine."

I don't look up at his words.

His right arm crosses over his body, and his finger hooks the side of my chin, turning my face toward him. We're millimeters apart.

"I don't hurt what's mine."

His lips are gentle, sweet.

"Punishments are harsh, and they're meant to teach a lesson. But they're earned."

My chin quivers, but I nod. Ajax and Andrew are not the same.

"I have a few more things to sort with the hunting lodge bookings, but then I'll go set up outside. You won't run."

"I won't run," I repeat.

His smile is breathtaking, and our kiss is loud. A giggle behind us makes me spin.

"Mary Lou, you are not dressed." Ajax frowns.

"Am too," she argues, tugging at her pajamas.

"You know what I mean." He sighs.

"Lulu said we can match," Mary explains, waving her denim overalls.

"I did," I defend.

"Don't encourage her." Ajax rolls his eyes. "I know when I'm beat." He holds up both hands and retreats backward to the table where his laptop still sits.

Mary and I share a smile.

"Trade?" I ask, holding out the books.

Mary nods, passing me the overalls.

"Start with the math please, baby. Daddy will be over soon to do the reading."

Mary's face lights up at the mention of reading. I make a note to buy her a new book or two next time we're in town, right after I ask Ajax for the money. I cringe and glance at the man in question. Our eyes meet, his gaze questioning.

I lick my lip and turn away, shifting my attention to the ripped denim.

"Do you have a sewing kit?"

"Over there."

I follow his finger, refusing to look above his elbow. His sigh makes my eye twitch. Sitting with the supplies I need, I try to calm my nerves.

He's not Andrew. *No, he just murdered Andrew.* There's that twitch again.

I start threading the needle through the denim, and the large flower takes shape quickly. I stop every few minutes to help guide Mary through her assignments until Ajax joins her on the floor.

He picks a book and encourages her to start reading. I peek over at the two discreetly. My heart races, and my womb flutters the more I watch him with his daughter.

He's patient and encouraging, everything my parents weren't. Well, Greg Maxwell had been. I just didn't get to live with him for very long.

Ajax is many things, all bad and ugly, but he's a good father. My heart lurches again.

I could be pregnant, and the idea terrifies me for obvious reasons, but something deep inside me feels differently, and that scares me even more than carrying a serial killer's child.

Shit.

I hiss loudly, ripping my finger away from the needle. Blood beads quickly.

"Show me," Ajax demands, jumping up.

I don't get to deny him. His fingers are strong and confident as they squeeze the skin around my tiny wound.

"Ahh," I object, trying to pull away. At his look, I

immediately stop, shoving my hand toward him quickly.

"Better," he mutters. "It's not deep, but we'll clean it anyway." Ajax lifts my hand as he speaks. A gasp flies out of my mouth when the heat of his mouth surrounds my finger. He sucks the blood off, and my body instantly reacts.

Ajax chuckles as my body shivers. Why was that hot? What the fuck is wrong with me? His grin annoys me, and I let it show.

His short chuckle has me turning back to my project. I swallow an insult when his lips press into my hair.

"Okay, Piglet, back to the subject books, please. Daddy's going outside."

"Okay," Mary says, but her pout is anything but agreeable. One look from her and my annoyance at her father melts away.

CHAPTER TWENTY-SEVEN

Lulu

School doesn't last very long. Both Mary and I get distracted the minute I finish the repair. She insists on changing, which then turns into me changing. After all, I did promise.

Her subject books lay abandoned on the table as we sneak to the front door.

Ajax is busy placing plant pots a few feet away.

Weird.

I glance at Mary, but she just shrugs.

"Okay, thirty minutes playing near the stream and then back to math," I whisper.

Piglet nods her agreement.

Deal.

At the door, Ajax spots us immediately but feigns ignorance. I jump out of the RV over the steps, and

Mary quickly copies my actions. Straightening, we walk briskly toward the water, our backs ramrod straight. I hold in my smile as her little arms swing like she's marching.

She's so cute.

"Okay, Piglet, shoes and socks off. What are we hunting for first?"

"Fairies," Mary says in a tone that tells me she thinks that I'm a moron for asking.

We tuck our socks into our sneakers and step onto the large rocks. The shallow stream flows calmly.

Her laughter rings out, and I quickly lose track of time. The heat of her father's gaze fades the longer we're out here. He slowly goes back to what he was doing, then settles in a chair with his laptop on his knees.

Happy. I feel happy for the first time in a very long time. I push all thoughts of murder and Cromwell Town away and enjoy the moment.

"Girls! Mary, Lulu!"

I look around when I hear Ajax's frantic tone calling for us, but all I see are trees. *Shit, how did that happen?*

"We need to go back, Mary," I rush, offering my hand.

Please don't be too mad.

We hurry back to the stream. A worried Ajax stands on the other side. His face relaxes in relief.

"I'm sorry, we were playing," I explain lamely.

"I know"—he nods—"but it's time to come in." He waves at us to cross.

With Mary's hand still in mine, I reach out a foot for the first stone, only to panic. It's not there. I twist my head to make sure this is where we crossed earlier, and the same knobby tree is rooted behind us.

So where are the rocks?

Ajax's eyes drop to my bare foot still frozen above the flowing water. "Where are your shoes?"

I point at the two sets of sneakers close to him. "We used the large rocks to come over, but now they're gone."

"That can happen with streams."

What happened to not being mad?

"I'll carry Mary and wade across." I smile like it's no big deal. *It is a big deal.* The water isn't that deep, but the current has picked up, and I can see sharp rocks on the bottom through the clear water.

"You will not," he snaps, walking toward us and stepping into the water. His foot slips slightly, but he catches himself quickly. "It's sharp and uneven on the bottom, not to mention slippery," he grumbles. "Like I'm going to let my girls walk across it."

I blush at his words. After everything I've seen him do, those words shouldn't make me breathless.

He reaches us quickly. "Okay, hold on tight to Daddy's neck," he tells Mary as he crouches to scoop her up into his left arm.

Even with his earlier words, I'm not expecting him

to repeat the action with me, so I'm startled and scream, drawing the attention of nearby campers.

The mom of a family watching "aws" loudly, but Ajax remains oblivious, his complete attention on Mary and me.

His feet test the ground before he steps forward, the journey taking much longer than when it was just him.

"You were supposed to be teaching her science," Ajax reminds me.

"I was."

He raises a dubious brow.

I struggle to think of something to say. "Environmental science." I smirk.

Ajax throws his head back and laughs, making my stomach flutter.

His strong arm supports my weight, holding under my ass. Wiggling my toes, I dip them into the cold water.

"Behave," he warns, but the smile he gives me makes my own lips spread wide.

The three of us are back on dry land in minutes. I sit on the ground and help Mary with her shoes and socks before putting my own back on. I'm almost done when two very wet boots appear. The denim above them is dark blue. He's completely soaked.

I grimace. "Sorry."

"Did you have fun?"

I freeze for a second, wide-eyed. I don't know

what to say. Andrew would ask questions, and no answer would be right. Is this the same?

"Yes!" Mary answers for me.

Her father looks at me with a raised brow, waiting.

"Yes," I whisper with a nod.

"Then that's all that matters," he declares, clapping his hands. I flinch at the sound.

"Mary, baby. Would you please go fetch me a towel?"

The little girl runs full force toward the RV, more than happy to help. Once she's out of hearing distance, Ajax drops down to where I am.

"One day, you're not gonna flinch around me."

"You kill people," I reply, running my finger in the dirt.

His finger turns my face. "I won't kill you."

I gulp and lick my lip, my mouth suddenly becoming very dry. "But you will kill again."

"Yes," he answers honestly, "and I will teach our sons. Hunting is a part of me. I built a business of it. It's who I am. The fact that animals aren't enough for me has nothing to do with the type of father I am or the husband I will be."

My chin quivers at his words, tears breaking free.

"You feel this, this thing between us, Lulu. You can deny it until your last breath, but if you run, I will hunt you, and I'll kill anyone who stands in my way, anyone you spoke to, anyone who helps you. They'll die because of you."

I'm openly crying by the time he finishes, but I still lean into our kiss because Ajax is right . . . I do feel it.

CHAPTER TWENTY-EIGHT

Lulu

Tonight has been . . . nice.

My body feels heavy and worn out. Who knew running around after a five-year-old could be so tiring?

The heat of the fire warms me. The sound of wood popping breaks the silence every few minutes. The smell of burning marshmallows makes me open my eyes.

"You're on fire." I smile sleepily.

"Shit."

Ajax pulls his skewer out of the heat, blowing on the bubbling treat to put out the fire. It's black and crispy, but my mouth waters when he sandwiches the marshmallow with crackers.

Leaning over, he holds out the oozing treat. He juts his chin. "Open."

I do as told, moaning as the sweetness fills my mouth. "Mmm." I nod. "Even burnt, it's good."

Ajax laughs, taking his own bite. "Next one'll be better."

I blush at his wink. I shouldn't be this calm or this content, but I can't think of anywhere else I'd rather be. Only one thing could make this better. My eyes drift over to the bugs and the few fireflies near the tree line.

Fuck it.

Jumping up from my seat, I rush into the RV. Mary is fast asleep but not for long.

"Piglet," I whisper, brushing her hair back, "baby, wake up."

"Daddy?"

"It's Lulu," I say before gathering her into my arms. She's heavier than I remember.

Ajax is standing near the RV front door, completely puzzled. I smile, silently walking past him, and indulgently, he steps back.

I take Mary over to the bugs, swatting a few away when they get close to her face. "The fairies came out."

Sleepily, she raises her head. "They're bugs," she says groggily, resting her head back on my shoulder.

"They are." I nod. "They come out to guard the fairies while they play."

I feel her smile on my neck. Is this what it's like to be a part of a family? To be happy?

Slowly, I start to weave a tale of a princess fairy who was taken from her home by the fairy prince. "The fairy princess is scared, but she's trying to like her new home. It's hard because everything is new," I whisper, pointing at the flies that buzz around us. "Can you see her?"

"Uh-huh?" She nods, lifting her head and joining in. "She has pink wings."

I gasp. "They are. Oh, look, there's the prince. He's come to play, I think."

"He's very handsome and strong," Ajax adds. Warmth surrounds me as he wraps us in the blanket from my chair.

Mary giggles.

"He's not that handsome," I mutter to Mary, tucking the edge of the blue throw under her chin.

Ajax chuckles, his hand settling on my hip.

"Will she stay?" Mary asks.

"Hmm?" I blink, distracted by her father's presence.

"The fairy princess. Will she stay with her new family?"

"I don't know, baby," I answer honestly.

Piglet frowns, her eyes growing heavy. "The prince will be sad if she leaves. He won't have anyone to play with."

"He'll fix it, Piglet. He's already trying to give her a reason to stay. They'll be a family in no time. I'm sure of it, baby." Ajax slides his hand to rest on my lower stomach, and I can hear his confidence in his tone.

He already did. I wrap my other arm around Mary and shift her from my hip into a bear hug. I press my cheek to the top of her hair.

Something lodges in my throat at his words. I'm suddenly reminded of our unprotected sex. Would he take the baby from me? Threaten to keep us apart if I run?

I squeeze my eyes closed. It doesn't matter if I'm pregnant. He already has the ability to pull that card if he chooses. I love Mary as if she were my own. It's irrational and illogical, but I know without a doubt that I won't ever leave this little girl, even if it means taking her with me when I run.

Not that you want to leave.

I shove that thought to a dark corner of my mind.

"He wants her, and the prince gets what he wants, even if he has to take her first." His arms join mine around Mary so that he hugs us both. "She'll learn to love him back."

"What if she doesn't?" I ask.

"She will," he answers confidently, kissing the back of my head.

The rumble of a vehicle followed by a bang shreds our peace when a motorhome literally crashes its way into the parking area. It clips a tree with the left wheel but keeps driving as if nothing happened.

The driver turns out wide, then starts to reverse . .

. right next to us. *Really?* Three-quarters of the car lot is empty. I must have spent too much time with Ajax already because I shouldn't be this annoyed by someone being close to our RV. But of all the spots.

I gasp when Ajax tugs us backward, crowding us close to the side of our own vehicle. The motorhome swerves from right to left, and the driver is unable to keep it straight. My jaw drops when the back right wheel clashes with one of our camping chairs, leaving it flat and useless in its wake.

"Get her inside," Ajax rushes, anger and annoyance clear.

He keeps his large body between us and the still reversing motor all the way to our door. I let out a breath of relief when they narrowly miss the fire we were sitting around just moments before.

We could have still been sitting there! My eyes lock on the now dead seat. Ajax could have still been sitting there.

"Hey, neighbor," an elderly woman says far too loudly for the time of night as she climbs out.

While I barely smile, the man still guarding us openly glares.

"Oh, sorry about that. My Phil doesn't drive so good at night anymore. Damn cataract but he tries his best, and that's what counts."

"Not really," I whisper to the man next to me.

He gives a breathy laugh. "Put her to bed. I'll sort things out here."

I freeze at his words. *Sort things how?* As if he can read my mind, Ajax raises his brow.

"The fire needs putting out, and chairs need bringing in. Chair," he corrects with a shrug.

My shoulders relax.

Ajax smirks, giving my ass a firm pat. "I'll try not to kill them . . ." He looks at the ruined furniture. "But I make no promises."

I glare my disapproval but carefully climb the few steps into our RV.

Not funny.

CHAPTER TWENTY-NINE

Lulu

I wake up alone, shrouded in darkness. The other side of the bed is cold under my palm, making me frown.

What time is it?

The bedside clock reads 3:57 a.m. Curiosity gets the best of me, drawing me from under the thick covers.

Curiosity killed the cat, I remind myself. My legs are shaky as I stand, and my core gives a sharp twinge. We went to bed a few hours ago, but we didn't lie down to sleep for a long time, and we hardly slept. Why would he get up?

Pulling on his discarded T-shirt, I quietly open the bedroom door. Nothing, no movement other than me. I peek into Mary's room; she's fast asleep, one of her long braids hanging over the side of the mattress.

I huff a quiet laugh. I wish I slept that well. Silently, I close her door and head farther into the living area, but that's also quiet. He's not here.

My heart stops. *Please tell me he didn't go back for poor Phil and his wife.*

As if my legs have a mind of their own, I exit the RV, and my bare feet sink into the mud. It's gross, lodging between my toes. It must have rained after we went to bed, not that we noticed.

My core gives another twinge. Movement at the back of the RV draws me over. *Please don't be the elderly couple,* I pray. They seemed nice. Half blind and loud, sure, but nice.

Rounding the corner, I gasp. It's not the old couple. Instead, Ajax stands half naked, his bare chest splattered with mud and blood. The bottom of his jeans are filthy, his boots no longer black but brown due to the mud.

What really has my attention is the body at his feet. It's the guy from under the RV. My stomach roils.

Ajax's head snaps up at the sound I make when I see him. His face darkens. This isn't my Ajax. It's not the man who feeds me sticky treats or who plays with Mary—this is the man who killed my stepfather.

"Not a word," he hisses. I'm a statue forced to watch him bend, his long fingers grab the dead man's shirt, the body jolting when Ajax pulls, ripping a button off. I gag at the sound the body makes when he drops back to the wet ground.

Ajax stuffs the button into his front jean pocket.

I clamp my mouth shut, my nostrils flaring when he approaches. My whole body shakes, but I keep my feet rooted.

Fuck, fuck, fuck.

"You're supposed to be in bed, asleep."

I blink, my chest rising quickly. I want to say that I'm sorry, but I can't get my mouth to open.

"Is Mary asleep?"

I nod quickly.

"Good." He sighs, some of the tightness leaving his shoulders. "You will go back inside, lock the door, and stay in bed. I'll be in to punish you once I'm done. You should know better than to leave the RV by now, Louise. I'm disappointed."

His words pierce me. He might as well have used his knife.

A sound behind me has us both freezing.

"Too late," Ajax snaps.

He rushes over to where the body lies sprawled next to the spade and wafts the tarp wildly. He throws it over the corpse haphazardly as footsteps approach.

Ajax is in front of me again, his hands fiddling with his belt.

"On your knees. You're getting your lesson now."

I stare at him, stunned. *He's joking, right?*

Seeing that he's not, I obey, dropping down. My bare knees hit the cold, wet floor. The bulge in his trousers grows as he fights to free his erection.

Someone coughs. They're almost at the back of the RV.

Ajax's large hands frame my face, holding me steady as he shoves his cock against my lips. I keep my mouth clamped closed.

Pain hits my jaw. His thumbs press into the back of my jaw, forcing my mouth open. He tastes salty, the fat head of his cock disappearing to the back of my throat quickly, making me gag. The hands on my head draw me closer, burying my nose into his pubic hair.

I gag again. Ajax moans.

"Oh, my!"

I can't see who is behind me, but I hear rustling as they turn.

I try to tear my head away, but Ajax holds me still. His hips pull back a few inches, his heavy cock sliding over my tongue.

His panted breaths the only sound in the darkness.

"Phil," Ajax greets, like he's not fucking my mouth.

"I didn't see anything. My wife sent me out because she heard a noise." The old man rushes, "I'll tell her it's just some animals from the woods."

Ajax's chuckle is dark and husky. I can hear his arousal, not that I need to since the man is using my mouth like he used my pussy earlier, fast and ruthless.

"I'll turn her hearing aid off, you kids . . . well, good night." He stumbles over his words.

Ajax doesn't answer. Instead, his gaze drops to me. "Suck," he orders, "and watch your teeth."

My face flames under his palms, knowing that Phil probably heard his words. The air fills with sounds of what we're doing, and as my body responds to his rough actions, I glare up at him.

Ajax smirks down at me before pleasure rules him. His head tilts back, his mouth opening with a deep groan.

"Fuck," he pants.

My jaw aches, and my lips pull at the corners of my mouth as I struggle to swallow his thickness.

I wiggle, trying to relieve the tingle between my legs, and suck harder. His cock leaves my mouth quickly. Ajax and I stare at each other, panting.

"It's amazing what people don't see when you give them something better to look at." He grins, nodding to his right. I look over and see the tarp, and my stomach drops at the sight of a foot. The bottom half of his leg isn't covered.

I fall forward and gag again. This time, my mouth is empty. My hands barely support me, and the ground is slippery under my fingers. I wipe the back of my hand across my mouth and then my cheek, brushing away my tears.

Ajax fists my hair, tilting my head back and forcing my body to bow.

"You shouldn't have come out here," he tells me, shaking his head.

His hand wraps around his wet cock, the thick

shaft pointing straight at my mouth. I swallow, knowing what's coming.

"If it makes you feel any better, you probably saved his life," he says, nodding behind me where Phil disappeared. "But his eyes are shit, and he couldn't look away fast enough. Personally, I love the sight of you on your knees eating my cock. Open wide," he breathes.

I wince, widening my mouth as much as I can. He still barely fits inside, my teeth touching his hardness.

The hold on my hair tightens.

"Careful."

Ajax shoves in, then retreats all the way out. Over and over, he does the same thing. Fast in, slow draw out.

I'm kneeling before him, mud covering part of my thighs, the wet T-shirt tickles my upper legs, bunching at my hips. My tongue sticks out, waiting for him to slide back in, and I'm panting.

"I come. You don't," he orders.

Stepping closer, Ajax frames my legs with his feet, and his strong hands still my head. He fucks my mouth, his cock bumping the back of my throat over and over. I struggle to breathe when his hips are flush with my face.

Closing my eyes, I take what he gives me.

Pain and pleasure blur, entwining until they're one. This is the way it is with him every single time. And just like before, I'm practically crying with need. My body sings for him.

Disappointment and pride fill me when he gives a final gasp and a long groan. His cum shoots out, filling my mouth. It's thick and tastes bad. The thick liquid leaks out of the corners of my mouth and down my chin.

"Do not spit," he hisses.

My eyes widen, and I shake my head.

No, no, no.

Ajax pulls his cock free, but his hand slaps over my mouth. I try to turn my head away, but he moves with me, and I'm forced to swallow it down.

Satisfied that it's gone, he releases me long enough to tuck himself away. His hands grab under my armpits and lift me to my feet. My cries have turned to hiccups.

"Never leave my DNA somewhere that's not that RV," he orders, grabbing the bottom of his T-shirt I'm wearing.

He raises it, his hand pulling until he can use it to wipe my face—first my cheeks and then my mouth. The smell of mud and him fills my nose.

"Go back inside and shower. Leave this shirt on the bathroom floor, and I'll clean it with the rest of my clothes."

"Where are you going?" I manage through my hiccuped breaths.

"To finish what I started before I was gloriously interrupted." He grins, his eyes trailing lower to where my bare body is on display for him to see.

With one final wipe to my cheek, he drops the edge of the top and kisses my mouth.

"And don't even think about touching that pussy. You don't come again until I say so."

I hate him. I hate him. I hate him.

I chant on the way back inside, but I don't, and that's the fucking problem.

CHAPTER THIRTY

Lulu

"I want to match again," Mary declares, running into her dad's bedroom.

"Mary Louise, that door was closed. You know better," Ajax reprimands, pulling a shirt over his head. "Try that again, please."

"Aw," Piglet pouts.

"Do not encourage bad manners." He points at me from across the room.

"I didn't say anything," I defend, raising my hands.

"No," he agrees, "but that smile of yours says it all." He squints, glaring playfully and making my smile widen.

Ajax rounds the bed and pulls me into his arms before placing a gentle kiss to my lips. I get lost in the feel of him quickly, but the knock on the door brings me back to my senses.

One touch from this man and I forget who I am, who he is. I try to pull away, but he doesn't let me.

"Come in," he calls.

Mary opens the door dramatically, making me laugh.

"May I please come in?" she asks loudly.

"The two of you are trouble. It's a good thing I love you," he says, looking at Mary and then me.

I swallow the lump in my throat.

"Help Lulu with the laundry, please, and then it's time for school. I'll leave you ladies to it." He presses a kiss to each of our heads, then leaves the bedroom.

Mary's shoulders drop, but she joins me at the bottom of the bed without complaint. I pass her a T-shirt to fold. She fights with it briefly before throwing it onto the bed next to the piles of clean clothes I've already folded.

"I'll wear that today," she tells me.

I laugh, passing her another.

"Can we wear our overalls again today?" she asks.

"Mine are in the wash, baby. I'm sorry. But I laundered yours, and they're right there." I point at them hiding in the pile of clothes still needing to be folded and put away.

Mary's face lights up. "How did you know?"

"I had a feeling." I wink down at her. "How about you help with these, and then I'll see if Daddy will let us go explore for an hour this afternoon?"

"Deal," she agrees, grabbing a pair of my jeans from the pile.

Our deal hits a snag when it comes to her dad.

"Please, please, please," Mary and I echo.

I throw my head back and clasp my hands together, the same as the little girl at my side. Ajax laughs and closes his laptop.

"Well, you did do a full six hours without complaint . . . although that snack break took a good hour," he tuts.

"Please, Daddy," Mary asks.

"Alright." He grins, standing. "Let's go for a family walk."

Ajax helps Mary put on a jacket, then shrugs on his own coat.

"Shouldn't she have a coat on?" I frown, sliding my foot into my sneakers.

"She'll be running around as soon as we get out there, always does. Relax, Momma bear." He smiles, his hand grazing the small of my back. Leaning in, he gives me a loud kiss.

Mary waits by the door, her eyes watching us carefully.

"Let's go," I say in a singsong tone.

"If you think you're going out in November in just a dress without a coat, you have another thing coming."

"I'll be running around too," I tell him.

"Then a jacket will do just fine."

I don't think I have one out here. I grab his off the

back of the chair that he'd been working on, then make a big deal of pulling it on. It's massive.

Ajax is right, and Mary shoots off as soon as we exit, barely giving her dad the time to lock the door. He presses something on his phone screen and tucks it into his back pocket.

"Come here." He chuckles, lifting my arm. "Mary, don't go too far. Wait for us. Mary Louise," he adds when she doesn't listen.

Ajax rolls the sleeve up until my hand is free, one arm and then the other.

"Thank you."

"Go play. I know you want to." He gestures to Piglet.

I'm off before he even finishes, running to catch up with my new little buddy. We skip past the few families parked on the lot, waving and calling "hi" to random people.

We're close to the end of the lot, where the grass starts, when we say "hi" to another group of people. A few of them turn, and my face turns fire-engine red when I recognize Phil.

"Hey." His wife waves. "It's our new neighbors," she tells her husband with an elbow to the ribs.

His eyes widen under his thick-rimmed glasses. "Oh, um, hi," he mumbles.

"You guys, come on over and meet everyone." His wife smiles.

I'd rather be shot with an arrow in the woods.

"We're actually playing, but Ajax would love to

meet everyone." I grin, pointing at the man in question as he catches up with us.

His hands settle on my waist, holding me hostage. "Is that a fact?" He mutters into my hair, "You'll pay for that later."

I shiver at the threat. His gaze scorches my back as we leave him to the wolves. After yesterday, I make sure to stay within sight. Looking back, I see Ajax has been pulled into conversation with a few men. They point at a newspaper, then pass it to him.

Mary and I play near the water's edge but don't cross it today. Slowly, other kids join, some hunting for pretty stones with us while a few more play farther up on the grass.

"That's a pretty rock." I smile at one of the kids.

"Your mom's nice," the little blond boy around Mary's age says.

I wince, not knowing what to do. Should I correct him so that she doesn't have to?

"I know." Mary nods before I can decide. Her shy eyes peek at me from beneath her lashes.

I blink quickly. *Oh, Piglet.* I sit on the cold grass, watching them play, adding in words of encouragement when needed. Last week, my life was miserable, and my nerves were constantly on edge. How had I gotten here with this perfect family? Noise from the other adults filters into my thoughts.

Okay, so Ajax may not be perfect, but everyone has flaws. I roll my eyes, angrily pulling up pieces of grass.

"Mommy, can I go play over there with the other kids?" Mary asks, slowly approaching. Her little face screams anxiety. She's worried I'll correct her.

"Sure, baby," I manage to get out. "I'll be right there if you need me." I point at a spot under a tree, closer to where all the kids have congregated. Ajax won't be able to see her from where he is, but at least I'll be close enough to keep watch.

"Will you save my rocks so we can paint them later, please?"

"Absolutely."

Piglet holds my hand until we get to the spot I point at.

"I'll be right here," I repeat when she hesitates.

She starts to leave with her new friend, but spins back to me. Rushing over, she throws her arms around me and squeezes me tight. I hug her back.

"Right here," I whisper, stroking her hair.

She leaves me a mess, having no idea how much she just shredded my heart and fixed it with one hug.

I sit down heavily, emotionally wrought. How can a situation born of something so dark make me feel so much joy?

Andrew won't be the only one in hell, but at least Ajax will be with me.

I stay lost in thought, glancing up every few minutes. My fingers flick at small rocks and stones in the grass by my hips.

A pained cry makes my head shoot up.

Mary!

I scramble up and rush over. Mary is on her knees crying, her scratched hands look red and sore. Her new friend is crouched, patting her shoulder while the other kids crowd around. A few of the older boys are laughing.

I drop down in front of her. "Mary." I frame her face, wiping her tears with my thumbs. "What happened?"

"Mommy. I, he, I." She struggles to speak through her tears.

"He pushed her," the small boy tells.

My heart turns to stone, following his finger to one of the older kids. He's as tall as I am.

"Is that true?" I ask Mary.

She nods. I tuck my hands under her arms and help her to her feet.

"Let me see," I whisper, gently bringing her open palms closer. A few small stones are stuck to her skin. Softly, I knock them off and blow warm air onto the irritated skin. "We'll clean them, and Daddy will kiss it better."

"Okay," she hiccups.

"Are you hurt anywhere else, Piglet?" I whisper. My voice is as shaky as my body.

"My knee." Her words end on a wail when she looks down to see her newly repaired overalls ripped. The yellow and pink threads are loose, the flower distorted and ruined.

"Piglet," one of the teens laughs.

The redhead boy who pushed her starts to make oink noises, his friends joining in, and I snap.

Standing, I spin and advance quickly. The little shit doesn't react, just laughs more until I put my hands on his shoulders and shove him with all my might.

The prick falls heavily, letting out a sound close to a scream. His friends' laughter turns to him, and his face flames.

"Fucking bitch!"

"Consider yourself lucky it wasn't her dad, you little shit," I spit out.

My chest heaves, my breath catching. I can barely breathe. I gather Mary up into my arms. Every cry she gives breaks my heart.

"Come on," I say, holding my hand out for the little boy. He doesn't argue, and we head for the lot where the group of neighbors still stand.

"Where's your mom?"

He points at a beautiful blonde sitting on a lawn chair with a group of women next to where Ajax's group is. I escort him over, not letting his little hand go until his mom has a hold of him. Without a word, I walk through the group, past everyone asking questions, desperate to get my baby home.

CHAPTER THIRTY-ONE

Ajax

Rage and fear fill me like never before when I see my girls storming past the group.

I throw the paper down, all thought of the article about the search for the I-90 killer lost, and jump up in panic. "What happened? Is she okay?" I demand, my voice shaking. Piglet never cries like this. "Mary," I breathe, brushing back tendrils of hair trying to get a look at her face, but my little girl just clings to Lulu even harder.

"She scraped her knee," Lulu explains, her pace not slowing.

"My flower!" Mary wails.

"It's okay, baby, I'll redo it. Mommy will fix it."

My head rears back at the title. *When the fuck did*

that happen? Not that I'm mad, I wanted this, but I'm missing something. I don't like that. Not one bit.

I'm going to kill someone right after I fix this.

I curve a hand around Lulu's waist and rub Mary's back with the other. I need to touch them, to know that they're both here.

"Is anything broken?" I rush.

Lulu shakes her head, not speaking.

"Blood?"

She shakes her head again.

I breathe for the first time since I saw them. I'll take tears over blood and broken bones any day when it comes to these two.

I unlock the door quickly, then reach out and steady Lulu with a hand on her elbow as she takes my daughter inside.

Our daughter.

Mary's cries have calmed, but she still clings to Lulu, refusing to release her when she's set on the bathroom vanity in our en suite.

"I love you so much, Piglet. You're such a good girl. Daddy's going to clean your hands while we have a cuddle," Lulu tells her.

I move around the room, gathering the first-aid kit. "Can I see, baby?"

I have to nudge the back of her hand, but she releases her grip on Lulu's jacket, one hand at a time, for me to clean with an antiseptic wipe. Softly, I cover the irritated skin with antibiotic cream just to be safe.

Once done, I place a gentle kiss on each palm and declare them fixed. "All better," I whisper.

What happened? The words are on the tip of my tongue, but now is not the time to ask.

Lulu carries our girl to the bed. "Can you grab her some pajamas? There should be some in the pile from earlier in the corner. I didn't put them in her room yet." She ends on a mutter.

I gather the clothes and press a kiss on each of their heads.

Mary is almost completely calm now, but Lulu is still shaking. My baby's chin wobbles when she steps out of her overalls.

"They'll be just like new when I've finished with them," Lulu swears.

"Promise?" Mary whispers.

"With my whole heart."

I feel like a loose part. *What the fuck happened?*

"How about we put *Babe* on?" I ask, already heading for the TV. My girls are snuggled on the bed.

I picked right. Lulu is exactly what we both need.

A loud banging carries through the RV. It sounds like a sledgehammer on the front door. The rage coiling in my stomach starts to unleash. Finally, something I can do.

"Stay in here, and enjoy your film." I smile.

Lulu bites her lip, suddenly looking very guilty. Guess I'm about to find out what the missing piece of the puzzle is.

I give my future wife a dark look. I do not like surprises.

I shove the front door open, uncaring of who it hits.

"There better be a good reason you're hammering on my door," I growl, stepping out.

A large man, maybe an inch taller than my six-foot frame and as wide as a linebacker, staggers out of the way of the door. His face is as red as his hair, but he recovers quickly.

"That whore of yours put her hands on my boy," he roars, pointing wildly at the RV.

"The fuck did you just say?"

Oh, I'm going to enjoy this.

"Repeat what you just said," I order, stepping closer.

"Rob, please, let's just go back to the camper," his wife begs.

"No," he yells, ripping his arm away from her. "That bitch touched my son." He points at a teen who stands sniveling behind them. He's cradling his wrist to his chest. "Get her out here. She needs a man to teach her a lesson."

My hand wraps around his throat like a vise. *Where's a knife when you need it?* I imagine sinking it between his third and fourth rib before slicing it across the skin of his neck.

A calmness flows through me with the knowledge that I'll do just that one day.

He tries to fight me, but we're too close. He can't get a swing on any of his punches.

"You don't ever talk about my wife like that," I hiss. "She did that?" I ask the kid, nodding to his wrist.

He gives a frantic nod.

"Why?"

He looks at his mother for the answer.

"I didn't ask her. Why?"

"Because I pushed the kid." He shrugs, and my blood freezes. "She was being annoying. Her and the other brat were running around, so I just tripped her a little, and then her psycho mom came and pushed me over. Everyone laughed, fucking bitch." He's nearly crying again.

I release my hold on his dad's neck and latch my hand onto his shoulder instead. Pulling forward, I bend him slightly and deliver a punch to the solar plexus. Air shoots out of him.

"Looks like it's your family who needs a lesson."

"He's fifteen years old. She's a grown woman," the wife defends, pointing behind me.

I was wrong. His family members aren't the only ones. Lulu is in need of another lesson. I don't glance back. I know better than to look away from a threat, even one gasping for air.

"Is it true? Did you hit him?" I ask Lulu.

"Yes," she says, her voice shaky. "But he deserved it," she declares, her tone now confident.

"He's a child!" the boy's mom yells.

"And she's a little girl. That boy is almost bigger than I am, and he thought it was funny to push her to the ground. He deserved what he got, and I'm not sorry." Something tells me those last words were for me.

"Go inside," I tell her calmly.

I fill with pride when I hear her do it.

"You heard her. He deserved it. Come to my door again, and this won't be a polite conversation."

"This isn't over!" the large man says, but his threat carries little weight when his wife has to help brace his weight for them to leave.

Lulu hit someone to protect my kid. *What am I going to do with her?*

Chuckling, I scrub my face. I know exactly what I'm going to do with her.

Marry her. Right after I fuck a baby into her.

I close and lock the RV door quietly. "Mary?" I ask calmly.

Lulu chews her lip, pointing at the bedroom.

"Words, Lulu."

I fiddle with the leather in my hand, drawing her attention. Her eyes double in size at the wallet in my hand.

I raise a brow expectantly, waiting for her answer. I open the wallet and take out the prick's driver's license. *Jett Meadows. 849 Clover Street, Jackson, MS.* Looks like we're going to Mississippi for the new year.

I place the card back and throw the wallet down

on the kitchen island. The sound of the leather slapping down makes Lulu flinch.

"In your bedroom, she fell asleep. I wanted to see what was happening out there, but I left the film on in case she wakes up," she rushes.

"She won't," I say, walking closer to Lulu, who backs away into the kitchen area. "Our bedroom."

"What?" she breathes, her eyes glued to my hands that are now unbuckling my belt.

"You said my bedroom. It's our bedroom."

"I guess." She shrugs, still backing up.

"You guess?"

Lulu shrugs, her eyes finally meeting mine.

"Lower your panties and bend over the counter."

"Ajax . . ."

"I won't repeat it."

Lulu turns, then takes the two steps to the kitchen island. Her hands shake as she reaches under the skirt of her dress. The black cotton panties drop to her knees, her ass lifting as she positions herself how I want.

"You assaulted someone to protect our daughter?" I ask.

I watch the back of her head move as she nods. The reflection of her face in the oven to our left shows me her face is screwed up, her eyes closed as if she's bracing herself.

I drop to my knees behind her and gather her skirt, the red material drawing me in like a bull.

"I have never, ever been this hard. Never felt this

kind of excitement, not even when I hunt my prey. You were fucking made for us," I declare right before I dive in.

Lulu squeals, shocked.

I eat her pussy with vigor. I stab my tongue into her, showing her what's to come. I bite at her clit and folds, sucking down the juices that leave her.

My bride-to-be cries out as she comes over and over, but I don't stop. Her legs shake more and more with each release.

"Please, I can't. I can't," she begs.

My cock leaks, begging to fill her. I stand to my full height and shuck my pants down just enough to release my thick prick, then anchor my hands on her hips.

"You were made for this family. You're never leaving," I whisper, and then I fill her. One shove forward and her body swallows my dick.

My hips slap against her ass, the sound filling the kitchen along with the undeniable smell of sex.

Lulu cries out. Her pussy clings to my cock with a viselike grip. She's so close.

"Someone might see," she moans out.

"Good," I pant. "Let them watch me fuck my wife," I taunt in her ear. I lick at her jaw, biting as I go. "Let them watch me pump my child into her womb. Watch her beg me to fill her with my cum."

I lean back and smack her ass, slamming my hips into her harder.

"Beg me," I yell.

"Ah, ah, ah." Lulu gives a small cry every time I bottom out inside her.

I smack her ass again. "Beg me!"

"Fill me! Please, Ajax, fill me."

I come with a roar, my thrusts mean and erratic, and our bodies squelch as I fill her with everything I have. Lulu's body grips me even more, ripples of pleasure rolling over my shaft. Her whole body shakes as she rides her last orgasm before collapsing weakly onto the kitchen countertop.

I pant, bracing my hands on each side of her head, my cock still buried deep.

"You're never leaving."

CHAPTER THIRTY-TWO

Lulu

"I'm sorry that we have to leave."

Ajax pauses in collecting his plant pots to look up at me. "Never apologize for protecting our kids."

Kids.

Mary suddenly feels heavy in my arms. Setting her on her feet, I stroke the back of her hair to calm her. The girl's been glued to me ever since she woke up from her short sleep.

Ajax reaches into his back pocket and takes out the wallet that he stole earlier. He takes another look at the driver's license, then tosses the whole wallet under the camper next to us.

I shake my head, silently begging him not to.

"Is there anything you'd like to do today?" Ajax asks, ignoring my plea.

"Maybe go get Piglet a new book?" I suggest, smiling at her.

"Please, please." She bounces.

"We can drop into one of the towns on our way back to the I-90." Her dad grins. "Right," he exclaims, dusting his hands off, "let's get out of here before your momma gets arrested for assaulting a minor."

I don't return his grin.

Asshole. I tilt my head and glare. *Shit, I hit a kid.*

"He was practically an adult, just you know . . . younger," I huff, walking inside.

Ajax laughs, lifting Mary over the steps. She quickly scampers after me.

"I want to sit with you," she rushes.

We head off quickly. Mary and I kneel on the sofa, waving to Phil and his wife when we pass them while walking. The older lady responds, but Phil squints until she says something we can't hear.

Phil waves back quickly, but his wife turns his arm to show us where we have moved past them.

"Blind as a bat," I mutter, making Mary giggle.

We play I Spy all the way to town. Large buildings start to sprout up as we leave the rural peace and quiet. I've been with Ajax and Mary for a week, and the thought of being in a town makes me squirm.

"I hate parking this thing in town. It stands out like a sore thumb, not to mention how hard it is to find space," Ajax grumbles, climbing out of the driver's seat.

"We'll make it quick," I promise, already wanting to leave.

I help Mary into her coat and blush when Ajax holds mine out too.

"We're parked in the bus station parking lot. There's a small bookstore over the road." He kisses me, pulling a cap down over my head.

"Keep your head down when you're in shops."

I nod.

The parking lot is half full, but the street is packed with people because of some kind of town event.

Ajax groans. "Hands," he demands, holding his arms out. Mary and I each take one. I wiggle my fingers until he lets me entwine them with his.

The warmth of his palm helps to calm my racing heart. Other families smile in greeting as we weave through the crowd.

"Oh." I stop outside of a Target. My arm pulls to the right, Ajax and Mary still walking, until he notices I'm not following.

I point at the store. "Please." I smile.

"Mom wants to go this way," Ajax declares, redirecting our little group.

We walk down the aisles browsing, not really looking for anything. A dye kit grabs my attention.

"Can we get this?" I ask Ajax. "Mary has a white T-shirt. We could make matching tie-dye tops." I smile at Piglet.

"I have a white shirt somewhere too. Maybe we can do a family craft thing. I want to match my girls."

Mary and I nod excitedly.

Slowly, we throw other things into the cart as we move throughout the store. Cookies, chips, a board game, a doll, new slippers, and a giant box of gold fish crackers.

We walk down the toiletry aisle last. "I need tampons," I explain, stepping away.

Grabbing my favorite brand, I add them to the cart.

"Or not." Ajax smirks, throwing three pregnancy tests in with them.

My mouth moves silently, at a loss of what to say. Ajax kisses me quickly, not wanting a scene. He claims my hand again and pulls us down to the checkout.

"Piglet, do you want anything else?"

The little girl looks around until she spots something.

"A ball, please."

"After what happened last time, how could I say no? But it goes in the bag until we're in the RV."

"What happened last time?" I ask.

"You." Ajax grins, putting our stuff on the conveyor. "You sure you don't want to get your books from here?"

"No." I shake my head. "I'd rather go to a small bookstore. The small-town girl in me, I guess." I shrug.

Mary and I play with her new ball until everything is paid for. Ajax opens the bag, nodding into it.

Piglet scrunchies her nose but deposits the bouncy ball inside.

"Let's go get a new bedtime story." I clap.

"Do you read?" Ajax asks.

"Sometimes." I shrug. "I prefer TV. You?"

"Same. Although I enjoy doing other things with my evenings as you've learned." He winks.

I blush, covering my face. Ajax pulls me closer when we step out of the store. The bag taps my legs as we walk, and his other hand holds Mary's tightly.

"Can I buy it?" I ask meekly.

He gives me a puzzled look.

"The books," I elaborate.

"Of course you can." He nods.

I clear my throat, feeling embarrassed. "I, um, I don't have any money, Ajax."

He frowns, realization dawning. "I'm sorry." He releases me and switches the bag to his other hand to reach into his back pocket and pull out his wallet. He hands me two twenties outside of the store.

"You're staying out here?" I ask, shocked when he leans against a parked car.

"You girls go bond, but I'll be watching."

I swallow hard and nod.

"Let's go book shopping, Piglet." I smile, holding out my hand. "You're being very well-behaved, baby girl."

Mary Lou grins at the compliment.

"What are you thinking? Fairy tale, animals, maybe some witches or wizards?"

"I want a book about fairies this time. A princess fairy."

"Have you read *Harry Potter* yet, or do I have to wait a few more years for that?"

"No, I saw it advertised once, though." She shrugs.

I gasp. "You've not watched the films either?"

Piglet shakes her head.

"Well, we need to fix that. I think I can talk Daddy into a few film nights where we stay up super late and snack until he has to carry us both to bed."

Mary laughs. "Yes, please."

"Okay, let's grab the first *Harry Potter*, and then we can take our time finding that fairy book."

We lose track of time quickly. Even sneaking into a corner at the back of the shop to sit and read some of the shorter books.

"Hopefully, your dad wasn't too bored." I wince at the counter.

Stepping to the right, I strain my neck. He's still standing on the sidewalk. He's moved a little farther away to read a newspaper on sale.

At least he's entertained. Now I feel less guilty.

"Thanks for shopping here today." The clerk smiles, handing me my change and our bag.

I eye the coins in my hand and make an impulsive decision.

"One more stop?" I check with Mary.

My sweet girl smiles, more than happy to follow

me around. Exiting the shop, I make a beeline for the curb, my target on the other side of the street.

I keep Mary close as we walk quickly, avoiding everyone rushing past us. We really picked the wrong day.

"Can you hold that for a second, please?" I hand Mary the bag, which she readily accepts. I tuck her in front of me so she can't wander off.

The quarters make the pay phone click as I push them in. I press the number of my best friend quickly; I only have time for one call. I'm hoping for voicemail, so I pick the friend that I know won't answer.

"Hey, Sam, it's Lulu. I just wanted to reach out and tell you not to worry. I'm sorry that I left it so long between our calls, and I canceled all the time. Life just sucked. But I just wanted to say that I'm okay. I'm safe, and I'm happy," I whisper into the phone. "I love you. Tell Shelby I love her too. Bye, Sam."

My heart aches, knowing that I'll never see them again, but I have something else now, something better.

Mary smiles up at me. "Mom, can I have some cotton candy?"

I follow her pointed finger and check what money we have left. Just enough.

"Sure, but we have to be quick. Daddy's waiting." She hands me the bag and takes off running to order her cotton candy.

"Mom, quick, we've got to hurry." She waves me over.

I don't think I'll ever get tired of hearing that name.

CHAPTER THIRTY-THREE

Ajax

I turn from the newspaper stand, a flash of blue catching my eye.

Another cop car. That makes three that have driven by. We're close to the I-90, too close. We shouldn't be here shopping. I need to be more careful. We have Lulu with us now, and she's more likely to be recognized. Cromwell isn't far enough away for my liking.

Something tickles at the back of my mind, urging me to turn. My breath catches as I do, blood draining from my face. I walk toward the woman in the black pantsuit.

Agent Collins. FBI are here. How the fuck did they know? I didn't even know we were coming here.

I'm not risking getting stuck in another roadblock. We need to leave now.

After years of tracking the I-90 killer, the FBI have never gotten close to me in their search. That's not about to happen now.

I watch, unable to look away. The local police look annoyed and tired.

I guess Agent Collins makes friends wherever she goes. The man at her side draws my eye. Special Agent Aaron Mitchell, the man in charge of hunting the I-90 killer. And he does not look happy.

His upper lip pulls back in a snarl, the angry words he spits out lost in the noise of those around us. Agent Collins flushes, her gaze fixed on the finger he's pointing at her face. The older man straightens, standing to his full height.

His eyes stay on his agent as he waves away the locals without looking at them, his lips pinched tight.

Uniformed officers scatter, looking grateful for the chance to escape.

Not wanting to be seen, I turn away quickly. But my panic only grows at what I see next.

Fear and despair make me stumble.

Lulu and Mary step out onto the road, my new love smiling down at my daughter.

She's running and taking Mary with her.

Rage joins the swell in my chest. I rush forward, desperate to get to them, but people block the way. I push through, shouting for her to stop, all thoughts of police momentarily forgotten.

"Louise! Mary!"

I lose sight of them when traffic picks up. Cars, trucks, and buses hide them from sight. I can't see my girls.

This isn't happening.

A large bus stops directly in front of me as the traffic stills on one side. The other continues to flow, keeping me trapped on this side. I stand on the curb, gasping for air as my whole world crumbles.

I can't live without them. I won't.

The bus hisses, the noise making me jump as it pulls away.

Mary and Lulu stand on the other side. My baby girl waves excitedly with cotton candy clutched tightly in her hand, the other holds Lulu's.

Wide-eyed, I take in their matching smiles. My gaze flicks behind them to the cotton candy stand surrounded by another family. My gut twists at the pay phone beside it.

What did you do, Louise?

My body turns, a mind of its own, to where the feds and local cops still congregate within the crowd. Lulu's gaze follows mine. *Does she see them?*

My wife-to-be and daughter step out into the road as the cars thin. My heart thuds with every step they take. I'm having a stroke at thirty-six.

My girls cross quickly, but it feels like a lifetime. Their big smiles attack my chest, taking away my panic as they come back to me. As Lulu comes back to me.

My eyes glance at the bus station behind them. She had time, and she had Mary. This could have ended so differently.

But it didn't, I remind myself.

She chose to stay. Lulu chose us.

CHAPTER THIRTY-FOUR

Lulu

When I cross the street, my smile falls at Ajax's expression.

He's angry. Shit. I knew we shouldn't have gone that far, but I couldn't leave forever without reaching out to my friends. Before Ajax and Mary, they were the closest thing I had to family. I was just too deep in denial to see it.

"What's wrong?" I ask, feigning ignorance.

"Absolutely fucking nothing." He sighs. His whole being relaxes as we join him on the sidewalk.

Ajax drops his forehead to mine, and his deep frown transforms into a bright smile, his hands gentle as they frame my face.

His body shakes, the tremors traveling up his arms and into my body. *Not so relaxed.*

His kiss makes me moan. "Hi," I breathe against his lips. "We just wanted candy." I motion behind me with my thumb.

"How about we go home?"

"On to the next city?" I ask, our lips brushing.

"No. Home, home."

"Okay," I agree with a small smile. I blink up at him and squeeze Piglet's hand. "Let's go home."

CHAPTER THIRTY-FIVE

Lulu

The house is beautiful and very remote. The hunting business is miles away from the main house, so no one will be coming here.

Just me, Ajax, and Mary.

My hand drops to my stomach. We've been back for a few hours but are still emptying the RV. Ajax left to open the shed, ready to park it inside until the next trip.

"You okay putting your toys away while I do laundry?"

"Uh-huh." Mary nods, not looking up from her new doll.

"If you need me, I'll be in the kitchen or in the barn with your daddy."

"Okay."

I wait, but Piglet is happily brushing the doll's hair.

Well, okay then.

Trying not to feel rejected, I descend the wooden stairs. Both floors are spacious, and the rooms are wide. Mary has been attached to my side quite literally for the ten days it took us to travel to Wisconsin. The scenic route, Ajax called it.

But Mary was bound to settle down at some point. I peer back toward the stairs. I guess she wasn't the only one who needed the comfort.

I find Ajax in the barn, the building almost as big as the house. I eye the thirty-eight-foot vehicle, surprised to feel excitement at the idea of traveling again.

He stands at a wood unit, putting something from his pocket into an open drawer. He rubs another item between his fingers, then drops that in too. He does it a third time, and I peer into the drawer as I get closer.

Buttons. Hundreds of them.

"You collect buttons?" I frown.

"After a fashion." He smirks over his shoulder. "Mary?"

"Playing." I gesture back to the house. "It's really beautiful out here."

Ajax nods, reaching out for me with one hand while sliding the drawer shut with the other. His strong fingers raise me onto the countertop, then swipes the key from next to me and locks the drawer.

"I finished emptying the RV and found this," he

says, pulling a bag closer. The one from the store in Spokane.

I bite my lip when I see the pregnancy tests that he threw in the basket.

"I don't think it'll show yet, but I'd like you to take one."

I don't know what to say, so I say nothing. Ajax tuts, boxing me in with his hands on the wood surface.

"It's a big change."

I nod. *It is.*

"You'll love this baby just as much as Mary."

I nod again.

"And when he or she is here, I'm going to fill you again and again," he swears, his left hand planting in my hair. Fisting it at the back of my neck, he tilts my head as he wants. "We're going to fill that house with love and laughter. Forever," he says against my lips.

I want this just as much as he does. Ajax was right before. I'm made for this family. I'm made for him.

"Forever," I promise.

EPILOGUE

Ajax

My phone lights up, the security alarm screaming. I snatch it off the workbench and pull up the cameras.

Someone's on my property. *Not for fucking long.*

I grab the landline and dial for the main house. No answer. My anxiety kicks up a notch. Lulu is alone and at home with Mary.

The figure sneaks through the trees, avoiding the cameras that run along the dirt road leading to the house. I look around my work shed. There's only one thing to do.

Go hunting.

Excitement and trepidation course through me like a life force pushing me to run quicker.

Terror pumps in my blood. After everything we

went through to get Lulu to willingly stay, after everything that I did, I'm not losing her now.

No one is taking my family.

Jumping, I grab a thick branch and pull myself onto higher ground. I'm to the left of my house, next to the shed we use as a garage. I have a direct line of sight to my intruder.

I eye the tree line behind the intruder, but everything remains calm. No one else is here.

The weight of my bow comforts me as I ready the arrow. The world falls away when I have my prey in my crosshairs.

Three, two, one.

The arrow whizzes through the air, puncturing the target through the right shoulder. The force of it makes them fly back into the dirt driveway. A pained cry echoes out.

The fact that the threat is neutralized doesn't calm me. *What the fuck is she doing at my house?*

I jump down from my perch and check my camera. She's alone.

"Agent Collins," I greet, stopping by her feet.

Lulu chooses that moment to rush out of the house. "What was that scream?"

"Nothing to worry about," I reassure my wife.

She runs closer, gasping at the sight on our drive. "Oh my God. Ajax!" she cries, panicked.

"It's fine," I promise, stopping her advance with one hand on her back and the other on her belly.

Agent Collins laughs, the sound gurgling as blood

dribbles out the side of her mouth. "You're both going to jail, and that kid of yours is going into care," she pants.

Lulu covers her mouth, and horrified eyes find mine.

"Over my dead body," I swear. Keeping my eyes on Lulu, I press my boot down on Collins's knee, forcing it to the side until I hear a satisfying crunch.

She's not laughing now. The agent sobs, trying to reach for her knee, but it only tears at her shoulder that's pinned to the ground.

"Ignore her. Baby, go inside. Open all of the windows on the ground floor. I'll walk around the outside and close the shutters. Just like we practiced." I close the space between us to nuzzle my nose against hers.

"Should I lock the shutters?" she whispers.

"No, I'll come in after they're closed and secure the windows and doors."

"Backup's on the way," Collins hisses.

"No, it's not," I tell Lulu, not letting her look away. "Agent Collins arrived alone; she walked up through the trees. She didn't want to be seen and not just by us. You, Agent Collins"—I turn to address her —"are what they call eager to climb the ladder. No one is coming because you wanted the collar yourself," I taunt, nodding to where her gun lays. "No one knows you're here." I smirk.

The truth is written all over her face.

"Go inside."

Lulu sniffles, backing up.

"Well, let's get you settled before I secure the house, shall we?"

I take hold of the arrow in her shoulder with both hands and tear it out of her.

There it is. I tilt my head back and enjoy her pleas. No amount of begging will stop what is coming, but she can try.

I give her my back and grab her feet. Slowly, I pull her across the ground, leaving a trail of blood to deal with later.

"How did you find me?" I ask, pulling the rope down from the rafter.

"A guy in Cromwell that used to be a cop said he thought Lulu was dead like the others. The I-90 killer has been quiet lately, so I made a few calls. Turns out a marriage license was issued to a Lulu Clarke fourteen months ago, but I had to be sure," she groans out.

"Of course you did. Where is your car?"

I step forward and press my boot against her damaged knee. Her scream rings out, causing pleasure to coil in my lower stomach.

God, I've missed this. We don't travel nearly as much, and when we do, I keep my hunts hidden, buried in shallow graves off the I-90. *Except for the odd few,* I smirk.

"Just off the property!" she calls out. "There's a small road that leads to nothing but trees. I drove it in there so that you wouldn't see it," she sobs.

Hmmm, seems we need a few more cameras along the property line.

"Please, please," she begs.

Gagged and bound, I leave Collins in my workshop. The fun comes later. First, I need to protect my family.

I rush around the building, closing the shutters on every window. My cock grows harder with each shutter I close, one more second closer to a new hunt.

The inside of the house is silent, something that would normally worry me, but today it only means one thing . . . my family is in the playroom. The very soundproof and windowless playroom.

The padlocks are waiting for me on each windowsill.

Lulu did good.

I secure each shutter with a lock and then close and lock the window. No one is getting inside this house.

I crack the playroom door open, smiling at the sight that greets me. Mary is sitting at her small piano, playing a song for her brother. Lulu gives a half-hearted smile before settling Jaxson down in his crib.

"Ajax . . ."

"Shh," I stop her, leading her into the hallway.

"Are we safe?" she whispers when the door is closed.

"Very." I take her hand and lead her to the kitchen. "I'll fix this, but no one else is coming. Except me. I can't wait until after."

My wife blushes at my words, even after all this time.

"Bend over the table and lift your dress. This is going to be quick and rough. I'll make it up to you later."

I shove my pants down, freeing my cock. "Brace yourself," I warn.

When I thrust forward, we cry out as I sink into her warmth. My mind falls blank as I chase my high, knowing I have another coming soon after. The anticipation of a hunt only pushes me higher. Pleasure zips up my spine, reminding me that the thrill of a kill won't beat this. Having Lulu here, knowing that she's mine will always be the biggest high that I have chased.

One that I get the pleasure of reliving every day.

My soul settles. I have everything I could ever want. My wife, my family, and a terrified prey waiting to be hunted and caught.

My life couldn't get any better, and it's all because of Lulu.

My wife, my love, my world.

Lulu

"Happy birthday to Piglet, happy birthday to youuu," we all sing out. Walking past the balloon arch, I place Prue on her play mat. The six-month-old kicks her legs, more than happy to be away from the noise.

"Your daddy and I got you an extra gift," I call over with a grin while my husband sneaks out of the kitchen.

"I want cake," William moans when I pass him.

"When your sister's ready," I tell him.

"But I'm hungry now," the eight-year-old complains.

I pass him an apple off the wooden side and smirk when he curls his lip. "That's what I thought. Sadie, you guard that cake from your twin, please," I tease with a raised brow at my son.

Rounding the table, I hug my oldest baby. "Happy birthday, Piglet," I say again.

"Thank you, Mom."

We stand in a tight hug until Ajax comes back. The gift makes the other kids gasp, and our oldest son laughs.

"Happy birthday, Piglet," Ajax says, his voice thick with emotion.

The baby pig wiggles in his arms, letting out a squeal.

Mary Lou stands still, her eyes growing bigger and bigger. "You got me a piglet." She's shaking, tears break free as she rushes forward to hold her new baby.

"He won't grow very big, but you're fully in charge of him. Food, cuddles, and poop." Ajax grins.

"Maybe you can use him as a test run for being a pig farmer."

"What are you going to name him?" I ask, rubbing her back.

"Babe," she sniffles, laughing.

"How are you going to kill him when you love him so much already?" Jax asks.

Mary gasps, covering Babe's ears. "No one's killing my child. Daddy, tell him!"

"That's what happens on pig farms. You sell them for meat." He shrugs.

"Jaxson," Ajax warns.

"I'm not saying it to be mean," he says, looking around at us. "Dad and I can help with that bit. Or," he stresses, seeing his sister is still upset, "you could have a farm full of lots and lots of fat pigs until they die of old age."

"Old age." Mary nods, patting Babe's head. "Kiss him," she demands to her brother, holding the piglet out. "Twenty-one times, for my birthday."

My son breathes in deep, his nostrils flaring. "He gets one, and I won't mention offing him again."

"Deal." Mary Lou grins.

Ajax claps him on the back. "Good boy."

Mary crouches, letting Sadie and Will pet him.

"Can we get one?" Sadie begs her dad.

"We have two dogs, four cats, six ducks, two horses, and now a pig. No, you cannot have another pet." Ajax laughs, wrapping his arm around my waist.

"Until one of them dies," Jax tries.

"Until one of them dies," his dad agrees, but adds, "of old age." Looking between the other kids.

"Can we show Prue?" Sadie asks her sister.

"Of course." Mary nods, heading over to the baby. Her siblings follow her like they have since the day they were born.

My heart melts.

"I want another one," I whisper.

"You know I won't say no, but after the trouble we had getting pregnant with Prue . . ." Ajax pauses.

"I know." The corner of my mouth lifts. "But we'll try?"

"We'll try," he promises, kissing the side of my head. "Do you think Mary will stay forever if I build her a little farm for her pigs on the land?" Ajax whispers, leaning in.

I pinch my lips to stop from laughing. "At least until she's thirty and needs more room for her pigs." I nod, encouraging him.

"Thank you," my husband says, pulling me close.

"For what?" I frown.

"For giving us what Mary and I needed."

I blink at his words. My fingers reach up to comb through his gray-streaked hair, "Well, it was only fair," I choke out, "you gave me the family I wanted."

I push up onto my toes, pressing my mouth to his. The kids talk loudly, and an argument over cake breaks out. I thumb my wedding band, and the inscription on the inside makes me smile into Ajax's mouth.

Forever.

Sixteen years ago, this man swore to never let me go. He failed to mention that he'd make my life worth living.

Ajax Whitler is a killer, a monster, an amazing father, and the only man I've ever loved.

Being taken was the best thing that ever happened to me.

The End

ABOUT THE AUTHOR

Jennifer Ivy is an author that loves to write dark romance.

The author can be found on several social media sites, such as:

Instagram; jenniferivy_author

TikTok; jennifer_author

Goodreads; Jennifer Ivy